A LOVE TO TREASURE

A LOVE TO TREASURE

Dee Wyatt

Chivers Press   •   G.K. Hall & Co.
Bath, England   Thorndike, Maine USA

This Large Print edition is published by Chivers Press, England, and by G.K. Hall & Co., USA.

Published in 2001 in the U.K. by arrangement with the author.

Published in 2001 in the U.S. by arrangement with Dee Wyatt.

U.K. Hardcover ISBN 0-7540-4387-8 (Chivers Large Print)
U.K. Softcover   ISBN 0-7540-4388-6 (Camden Large Print)
U.S. Softcover   ISBN 0-7838-9326-4 (Nightingale Series Edition)

Copyright © Dee Wyatt 1991

All rights reserved.

The text of this Large Print edition is unabridged.
Other aspects of the book may vary from the original edition.

Set in 16 pt. New Times Roman.

Printed in Great Britain on acid-free paper.

British Library Cataloguing in Publication Data available

Library of Congress Cataloging-in-Publication Data

Wyatt, Dee.
    A love to treasure / by Dee Wyatt.
        p. cm.—(G.K. Hall large print nightingale series)
    ISBN 0-7838-9326-4 (lg. print : sc : alk. paper)
    1. Large type books. I. Title. II. Series.
    PR6073.Y32 L6 2001
    823'.914—dc21   00–050067

674583

MORAY COUNCIL
LIBRARIES &
INFORMATION SERVICES

ʄ

CHAPTER ONE

'How much longer are you going to play this silly game of yours? I need my wife at home when were married Karen, not traipsing about all over the place—Sir James or no Sir James.'

Karen Muir's emerald green eyes glittered with hot indignation when she remembered their bitter row two nights ago. Sometimes, Malcolm irritated her to screaming pitch with his self-centred patronising, especially when he treated her job as though it was of such little importance that it could be brushed away like a bothersome fly. Something that he was magnanimously allowing her to amuse herself with until the time came for her to take up her rightful destiny—as his wife!

In the five years she'd worked for the Launceston and Broome Insurance Company, Karen had progressed from small investigations to the wider range of reclamations and conversions. Now this particular undertaking had been offered to her, and it was the biggest challenge of her career so far. Come what may, Karen was determined to prove to Sir James—and Malcolm—that she could handle it.

Hot and clammy from the long walk, she looked around and tried to muster some enthusiasm for the spectacular scenery broadening out before her. Her gaze roved indifferently over the crescent of white sand, and at the blue-grey waters of the Bristol Channel. Below her, half-hidden by the overhanging cliffs, bobbed a cluster of bright fishing boats riding at anchor in the harbour.

Under normal circumstances Karen would have been delighted to spend a few days in such a secluded paradise, but considering the reason for her being here, she could feel nothing more than apprehension.

She winced as her feet slipped on the small stones. The high-heeled shoes were useless on the steep path leading from Croesty Fach, and her tawny-red hair was beginning to stick in clumps to the back of her neck. Beads of perspiration had gathered beneath the large, tinted spectacles that shielded her eyes from the sun's glare, and the tip of her nose was already feeling sore with sunburn. The last thing she needed was for her feet to start hurting, too.

The path grew steeper and Karen paused for a moment beside a tree to catch her breath. She leaned her arm against a bough and the sun's light sent a myriad of fire-coloured rays from the diamond on her left hand. The engagement ring reminded her of Malcolm again and her green eyes darkened with doubt. Perhaps he was right. Perhaps she was crazy to come here.

She gritted her teeth. Just the mere thought of him at that moment, and the way he always seemed to doubt her abilities, spurred her on even more and she started off again.

At last Karen could see the house. As she drew nearer, rounding the bend, she spotted the crew of workmen working on a new section of building, and she picked out the brawny lankiness of the foreman she'd spoken to yesterday.

She'd asked him to point out Richard Marshall—the man she'd really come to see. But she had been told he was off on his boat somewhere and hadn't said when he'd be back. The foreman had shrugged indifferently, maybe tomorrow . . . and that had almost been the last straw.

Today, as she drew nearer, Karen could see that the foreman was not alone—there was another man by his side. The newcomer was leaning langorously against the building's door frame. He was tall, well over six feet, lean and broad shouldered. His hair was a tangle of black curls, long enough to cause him to brush a strand away from his eyes. His jaw was square and darkened by a couple of days stubble and, apart from a pair of old sandals, the faded, cut-off jeans were his only garment, leaving his torso and legs bare. His skin was the deep bronze colour that comes with long exposure to the sun and weather.

He turned at her approach and took a step forward. He moved with graceful agility and Karen, behind the shield of her glasses, squinted carefully at him, vaguely wondering why on earth she should be reminded of a dark panther.

She cleared her throat and called, 'Could you tell me if Mr Marshall's back yet?'

The stranger appraised her in amused arrogance, quirking a dark eyebrow at her brusque manner. 'Yes, he is,' he replied. 'I'm Richard Marshall.' She noticed a slight frown flicker across his brow and guessed at once that she was not what he expected.

Something happened to Karen then. Afterwards she was never sure exactly what it was. A strange feeling of recognition, of remembrance; a physical shock that sent waves, however fleeting, of what was to come. Karen was not prone to such imaginings. She liked to think of herself as practical, down to earth. And then it was over, the moment might never have occurred. She moved towards the two men.

'I'm delighted you've been able to make our appointment at last, Mr Marshall,' she said coolly. 'Even though you are a day late.'

He didn't answer right away. The look on his face said it all. It wasn't the first time she'd surprised a client by her appearance. And the fact that she was innately feminine, young, slender, and with long coltish legs had obviously thrown him.

She stepped up to him, her graceful body moving with a slight, unconscious sway of her hips until she finally stood before him, tilting her head upwards to look at him.

The man's night-dark eyes flickered over her face. 'You must be the person Sir James told me about, the one he said was coming to twist my arm into some crazy scheme he's been cooking up. Am I correct? Are you Miss Muir?'

She opened her mouth to reply but, before she could speak, he turned away briefly to answer the other man who was moving away. He nodded briefly then looked at Karen, adding as an afterthought, 'Were you comfortable in Croesty Fach?'

'Very comfortable, thank you. And yes, I am Karen Muir. I arrived yesterday . . . as arranged.'

He threw her an amused, arrogant glance, then merely shrugged and looked unconcerned.

'I'm sorry I wasn't here, but arrangements are flexible at Gwyn Radyr Fawr. You have to take things as they come.'

He looked as though he'd had a wealth of experience at doing just that.

Karen thought it would be very hard to imagine a man more at home with his environment. Everything about Richard Marshall smacked of his disregard for conventional society. Karen found herself wondering if it was wise to trust such a man with such an important assignment.

'Better late than never, Miss Muir,' he went

5

on with a laconic grin. 'And I must say, Sir James seems to be improving in his choice of staff.'

'Better never to be late. Mr Marshall,' Karen replied archly. 'The letter we sent was quite specific.' Her voice was low and a little husky, betraying a faint but unmistakable note of disdain. 'Did you forget that I was coming?'

'No.'

She waited for an explanation but none came.

Karen looked at him sharply, 'Mr Marshall, if you don't want the job you only have to say.'

'And what difference would that make?'

'We'll just have to find someone else.'

'It's a bit late now, isn't it? And what makes you think I'm not interested?' He turned and strode towards the house, leaving Karen no choice but to follow him.

'The fact that you weren't here yesterday for one thing,' she said sharply. 'We need a responsible man for this project, otherwise it can't succeed.'

'I don't suppose it has occurred to you,' Richard said mildly as he walked along the driveway, 'that I have other responsibilities besides waiting at the door to welcome you?'

'No,' she said frankly, struggling to keep up with his long strides. 'It hasn't.'

He startled her with his laugh. 'At least you are honest!'

Richard kept his eyes straight ahead, as he

strode well ahead, making further conversation between them difficult. Determined to keep up, Karen tried to match him stride for stride and as they neared the house she could see Gwyn Radyr Fawr clearly now as it loomed into view.

It was even more beautiful than she'd realised. It stood alone on the high cliff overlooking the bay, well protected from the rigours of the sea by its roof of green slates. The guest cottage where she'd spent the previous night lay far below them, hidden in the trees, and sheltered in a deep valley from the wind. Its pretty, slanted roof was just visible through the trees.

The walls were covered in ivy, and tall beechwoods lined the driveway, like a row of sentinels. Unexpectedly, disturbed by their approach, a family of crows lifted, cawed, and fluttered like ragged black streamers, then settled down again and the beech trees on either side of them were quiet once more.

The crows' sudden flutter caused her to flinch and, on impulse, Richard offered her his hand. Equally on impulse, Karen accepted it; their fingers touched and there it was again, the fleeting instant of recognition. Karen had to restrain herself from drawing away. She had never felt this electrifying jolt when she touched Malcolm.

She stole a quick glance at the man's good-looking profile. He looked around thirty, and he also looked as though he had known his fair share of women. She realised that working with him closely she would have to watch herself very carefully, because never had she experienced such an immediate and forceful response to a man.

She broke off her thoughts as Richard automatically quickened his stride, taking the rest of the path quickly and dropping her hand. 'Why didn't they send the other chap . . . Lovell?' he demanded brusquely as they at last entered the delicious coolness of the house.

'I've no idea,' she answered tersely. 'Perhaps they believed that I would be better suited to the job.'

Richard paused in the entrance hall, his dark eyes narrowed. His gaze swept over her challengingly in a move that she felt was intended to put her in her place. Karen looked back at him unflinchingly. Her experience, fostered by years of power struggles with her male colleagues, did not desert her. Nothing could be discerned from her expression except absolute determination.

At length, his gaze dropped, but before she could relish her victory, he went on quickly, nodding and gesturing eloquently towards the sitting-room door, 'After you, Miss Muir.'

She inclined her head very slightly and went past him into the room. 'Now, Mr Marshall, let's see it you have all the facts—'

'Look,' he glanced quickly at his watch, 'I'm

afraid discussion's impossible right now.' He had followed behind her as she had entered the room, and was standing so close to her now that it gave her a small shock as she turned to face him. 'I have a few things I need to sort out here first, so I'll have to leave it for say, an hour. In the meantime, make yourself at home and I'll get Mike to bring your things up from Croesty Fach—you may as well stay here tonight.'

'That's very kind of you, but I must get this assignment started, and as soon as possible.'

'What difference would a few more hours make?'

She gave an exasperated sigh. 'A great deal of difference. Every moment we waste is not only very expensive to my company, but it also puts the project in danger of being discovered—and ultimately that means failure!'

He raised his hand to push away a lock of hair from his forehead. He had nice hands. Hands that looked as though they wouldn't be afraid of hard work. 'You seem quite serious about this little game of Sir James's.'

'It's not a game!'

He pursed his lips. 'So it would appear.' His dark eyes were smiling as he added quietly, 'But there's not a lot we can do about it today, is there? And I have to sort something out with Mike before I can do anything else.'

She took a small step back and inhaled

sharply 'Who's Mike? Sir James gave me the impression you lived alone. No one else must know of this assignment.'

Richard smiled cynically. 'Then I won't tell anyone if you won't.' He swung away laughing, striding down the hall leaving her to wander at will through his beautiful house. That was obviously the best she was going to get today.

Half an hour passed, then fifteen minutes more. Karen moved impatiently around the elegant sitting-room, glancing now and then through the long windows opening out on to a superb view of the sea beyond.

She was irritated by Richard Marshall's manner. Karen had spoken the truth when she'd told him that punctuality counted heavily with her. But, as she looked about her, she saw the absurdity of counting precise moments in this wonderful place.

Five more minutes passed. She toyed with the idea of walking back down to the beach and letting Richard Marshall cool his heels waiting for her. It was only the suspicion that he wouldn't care where she was that stopped her. Instead, she began going through the papers she had brought with her, studying them once again even though she knew them by heart.

A shadow fell over her shoulder causing her to look up. Richard had come in through the open French window and was standing directly behind her. 'Sorry about that,' he said. 'It took me longer than I thought to find Mike.'

Karen smiled coolly. 'Did it? I hadn't noticed. It's so beautiful here.'

Richard shot her a swift glance. The look in his eyes questioned if she was being serious.

He turned away quickly as a man came through the door. The man was short with a heavy, round stomach and his frayed check shirt flopped over the waistband. His legs were slightly bowed and his greying hair hung limply over his ears. 'Miss Muir's room's ready now, Mr Marshall. I've taken her bags up and switched the hot water on.'

Richard Marshall stood up and moved towards an ancient rolltop desk, which was overloaded with dusty papers and books. 'Thanks, Owen. Give this to Mike, will you? He's waiting down by the jetty—he knows what to do.' He handed the fat man a piece of paper. Owen shuffled out of the room and Richard turned back to Karen.

'I'm sorry about the state of the upper room, Miss Muir, but as you will see, we're in the throes of conversion. I realise you must be used to more civilised surroundings.'

'Is this the only house on the island?' Karen asked.

'Yes, apart from my guest cottage, Croesty Fach. But, in spite of the present upheaval, this house is infinitely more comfortable, as I'm sure you'll find out. Your room is the last one on the right on the first floor.' He gave her a brief smile and crossed to the door, pausing as he reached it to say, 'I'll see you at dinner then.' And then he was gone.

She was surprised to find her room was large and tastefully furnished. Certainly an improvement on the one she'd slept in last night at Croesty Fach, which had held a single old-fashioned bed and a dressing-table that had seen better days. This was certainly more to her taste.

Karen sat down in the soft leather armchair by the open window and kicked off her shoes, her eyes taking in the pastel colours of the walls and carpet. Back in her office she'd read about the proposals Richard Marshall had sent in for Gwyn Radyr Fawr, and she could see now that it would make a splendid tourist spot for sailing enthusiasts, located as it was with its natural harbour and the sea almost on the doorstep.

Everywhere was in the process of change. Outside the window she could hear the hammering of the workmen, and when she had found her way along the wide gallery on the first floor, she could see that rooms were being torn apart ready to receive their first influx of holidaymakers.

Karen undressed quickly, and wrapped in a kaftan, she went out along the passage, stepping gingerly over pots of paint, ladders and stacks of sweet-smelling wood until she found the bathroom. The shower creaked ominously when she turned it on and the water gushing from the spray was the colour of earth. Pipes rattled and gurgled, and the floor under her feet vibrated to such an extent that she had a horrible vision of a boiler somewhere about to explode.

She let it run for several minutes, until it was fairly clear, then stepped under. It was blissfully cool on her skin and she soon felt wonderfully refreshed and clean.

After she'd showered, Karen returned to the bedroom and slipped on fresh underwear, a linen dress and tied a bandana around her long, damp hair.

Her earlier bad humour was fading fast and she allowed herself to feel grateful for the position of trust that had brought her here.

The birdsong outside her window made her smile, and the cawing and fluttering of wings startled her as she opened the window a little wider. The sky was clear and blue, the air fragrant with the perfume of wild flowers and the tang of the sea.

The rumble of her stomach broke into Karen's perusal of the trees and, following her nose, she made her way downstairs to the dining-room where Richard waited.

He still hadn't shaved but gone were the casual denims, replaced by an elegant dark suit and he stood by the fireplace, glass in hand, moving to meet her as she appeared in the doorway.

'Sorry about the bathroom,' he murmured as he held her chair. 'I hope you were able to manage fairly well.'

'Perfectly well, thank you.'

He sat down at the opposite side of the table and flashed her a quick, brilliant smile. 'You must be hungry.'

She merely smiled politely and said, 'Yes, a little.'

The grilled lemon sole was delicious and she devoured it hungrily. It was served by a stout woman whom Richard introduced as his housekeeper, Mrs Williams, and whom Karen took to be Owen's wife.

After dinner, she followed Richard into the sitting-room. She was impatient to be getting on with her assignment. Time was of the essence on this job.

Karen sat on the wide sofa and turned her green eyes to Richard. 'If you're quite ready I'd like to talk about work now,' she asked, hoping she sounded more businesslike than she felt. 'Unless, of course, you have more important things to do.'

Richard turned to her with a smile. There was no denying he was a most attractive man. 'I'd rather leave our discussion until morning. What do you say to a nightcap instead? We can talk about work tomorrow.'

'Well . . . all right,' she agreed with a small shrug. 'Perhaps it is a bit late. But first thing in the morning, we start work, Mr Marshall. We

14

cant afford any more delay.'

He splashed a little soda into two rather large brandies and handed her one, easing his long body comfortably beside her. 'First thing after breakfast, I promise, you shall have my undivided attention. Now, tell me about yourself, Miss Muir.'

'It's Karen. If we're to work together I'd rather you called me Karen—it'll save time.'

He then grinned. 'I agree, and you must call me Richard. Now that's settled, I'll own up and tell you that you're not what I expected.'

'Really?' Karen acknowledged politely, not at all sure she was ready to hear more.

Richard paused, smiling at her. 'What I mean to say is that you're far too attractive to be connected with something as dull as insurance.'

Karen found herself smiling back. 'Yes, I suppose we all have our preconceptions,' she conceded.

How strange that a man's smile could change his appearance so drastically. She had the distinct impression that he rarely smiled and when he did it was almost with a reluctance.

She noticed him glance at her ring. 'Does your fiancé approve of this job of yours?'

Her left hand moved involuntarily, suddenly defensive. Why, yes . . .' she lied. 'Of course he does.'

'Then the man must be a fool.' His face

15

showed a hint of bitter humour.

Karen's green eyes glittered dangerously. 'I don't need your approval.'

He gave a slight laugh, a deep pleasant sound and the bitterness she'd seen in his face only a moment ago seemed to fade away. 'I'm sorry,' he said softly, turning to look at her, 'I asked for that, didn't I?'

Karen studied him, noting the unrelenting strength of his mouth. He looked the sort of man who would try to dominate, and he was not the sort she would want to get involved with, even if she was free to be given the chance. That was one of the things she liked about Malcolm. He was so safe to be with—so predictable.

He laughed again softly. 'Well, what conclusions have you drawn?'

Karen looked up quickly. 'What?'

'Now that you've had time to study me, what decision have you reached? Have you made up your mind already?' His eyes flickered mockingly over her face.

She stiffened. 'Is that what you think I was doing?' she asked coolly.

'Weren't you?'

'I'm interested only in getting on with the job I came here to do. Sorry to disappoint you.'

His dark eyes became serious. 'Of course,' he said smoothly, standing up and moving towards the drinks cabinet. 'Would you like

16

another brandy?'

'No, thank you.'

'I think I will—do you mind?'

'Of course not.' She studied him again as he poured more spirit into his glass and she sighed resignedly. She didn't want to get off on a bad footing with Richard Marshall, there was too much at stake. She couldn't afford to be ruffled by him—or he by her—so she switched gears as quickly as she could and cleared her throat. 'Well, now that we've got the pleasantries out of the way . . .' Even as she spoke she was aware of the underlay of sarcasm that had crept into her voice. 'Why don't you tell me what your plans are for Gwyn Radyr Fawr?'

'Certainly, if you're interested,' he agreed.

Karen listened attentively as he outlined his plans for the yachting marina. Before very long she found herself quite amazed at the professionalism of Richard Marshall, and more than a little impressed by his schemes and plans for his project. He'd certainly done his homework.

At her door he left her with a curt 'Goodnight,' and then turning abruptly, he strode down the corridor and into his own room.

Next morning, after breakfast, Richard led her out on to the terrace and, when they were seated, his manner was both serious and curious. 'Right,' he said, his night-dark eyes

17

resting on her face. 'As promised, you have my undivided attention. Tell me about this job. What is this thing that's so important to you and Sir James? What has he got lined up for me?'

'How much do you know?'

He shrugged. 'Not much. All I know is that Sir James wants me to justify postponing my work here and do some sort of investigation for him instead.' His good-looking face darkened into a glower. 'It had better be worth it, that's all.'

Karen glanced around carefully, confirming that there was no-one within earshot. Only when she was quite sure did she begin to explain what her company really wanted him to do.

CHAPTER TWO

Karen began quietly. 'About five hundred years ago, 1485 to be precise, a ship, the *Tudor Warrior*, set out from France carrying a valuable cargo—a fortune loaned by the French king to help Henry Tudor win the crown from the Yorkists.'

He gave a dismissive sigh. 'Not that old chestnut again.'

Karen ignored his jibe and went on, 'We believe the ship went down somewhere around here. We think it may be lying off that other island of yours, the little one, Gwyn Radyr Fach.' She glanced at Richard, waiting for his comment, but his only reaction was to sit back in the chair with a resigned look in his eyes. She went on, 'The *Warrior* was due to arrive at Milford Haven with the rest of the Tudor's fleet, but we know for a fact that there was a bad storm and a lot of ships were lost.'

'We also know that some survived, but they were blown off course and it was months later when some turned up in other places— different harbours along the coast. They've all been accounted for with the exception of one, the *Tudor Warrior*. It was generally believed at the time that it went down with all hands, along with the cargo.'

'So, what's new about that? We've heard the

story of the wrecks before.'

'I know. But it's a little different now. We have strong evidence that there were some survivors who managed to reach land, and they let the cat out of the bag where the treasure ship had gone down.'

'What kind of treasure did the French king provide for old Henry?' Richard asked.

'Gold coins. Probably worth around a million pounds or more today.'

'What makes you think the coins are still there?' Karen had the feeling he was not entirely convinced. 'How do you know the survivors didn't pocket them for themselves?'

She glared at him. Blast his arrogance, but she had a job to do. 'Well, of course I can't answer that, can I? But, according to our records, various attempts have been made to locate it over the years and, as far as we know, no-one's ever got anywhere near it. And there's no evidence to say that Henry Tudor received the shipment; not one of his records mention it, and if anybody kept all his money transactions well documented, he did.'

'So, where do I come in?'

'They're both your properties, aren't they?' His head nodded shortly so she continued. 'Well, we obviously need your permission to explore the seas around them, and it would seem that you're the only man Sir James believes is capable of finding it. The bottom line is, we want you to postpone your plans to turn your property into a holiday complex and lead the search for the coins.'

He looked at her incredulously. 'Postpone my plans for some wild scheme like this? The harbour's almost ready for extension. We need the good weather. If I leave it too long I'll miss next season as well.'

'You'll be well paid for any delay.'

Richard pursed his lips and shook his dark head slowly. 'It's crazy. A crazy, wild goose chase.'

'Sir James doesn't think so.'

'Well, I do!'

But even as he spoke she saw a thoughtful expression creep into his eyes. He sat, head bent, as though mulling over what she'd said. 'I had a sneaking feeling Launceston and Broome were a bit over-eager to handle the insurance on Gwyn Radyr Fawr,' he muttered, 'I thought they were more interested than usual in my ideas for a holiday marina.'

Karen smiled slightly. 'That's not the case— they are always interested in new business, and Gwyn Radyr Fawr as a marina would be worth a lot of money. It's just that you got in touch with us about your insurance more or less on the day when Sir James heard about the Tudor ship—pure coincidence.'

Richard gave a disbelieving snort. 'I'll bet it was! I know Sir James of old, from my army days, and I also know that the old boy can be pretty tight-lipped when he chooses to be—'

'Are you interested?' Karen demanded, cutting right in.

'Let's just say I'd like to know more.' He gave a sudden unexpected grin and added, 'I admit I'm intrigued.'

'Good! Sir James knows you better than you think, and these are your islands, and you know them—and the waters around them—like the back of your hand.' He nodded briskly and Karen went on, 'We know you've studied history and the fact that there may be a cache of Tudor treasure lying at the bottom of your stretch of water would naturally be of some interest to you.'

Richard's dark eyes narrowed suspiciously. 'Looks like you've been doing your homework on me.'

'We had to. And we came to the conclusion that if anyone could find it, you could. You've been on similar recovery operations before, when you did your stint with the marine commandos.'

He sat deep in thought, his eyes dark and brooding. He was so quiet that Karen wondered it he had forgotten she was still there. She almost made a move to get up and leave him sitting there, when he said quietly. 'You realise that the chances of finding it are extremely remote. If there's anything down there it's probably buried deep in the silt after all this time. How certain are you of the location of the coins?'

She unfolded a small map and pointed to a spot about ten miles west of Gwyn Radyr. 'We have ninety-nine per cent proof.'

Richard studied the area she indicated for a few moments, then he laughed incredulously. 'That's about the most formidable part of the whole area,' he said. 'It's impossible to reach unless you're a fish! Then there are the tides . . .' He shook his head slowly. 'Now I know you're crazy!'

'Nevertheless, that's been confirmed as the location.'

Richard stared at her steadily 'How? Has someone tried to reach it already?'

'No. We have access to certain . . . facilities.' She pulled a grainy photograph out of her briefcase and offered it to him. 'This is a high-altitude survey of the area. It you look there— Karen pointed to another spot, 'you'll see the shadow where the water around the rocks looks much darker than the rest.'

Richard studied the photograph carefully. 'Whatever it is, it's certainly lying deep.' He turned to Karen and smiled. 'This isn't from any plane, this is from a satellite. It must be a pretty big operation.' She made no reply but held his questioning gaze steadily as he asked, 'Are you sure you and Sir James are telling me everything?'

Karen nodded briefly. 'We believe it is big. We're not sure yet how big, so we want your permission to search . . . and, of course, your assistance.'

As she spoke she watched Richard's face carefully, waiting for his reaction. She wanted to see if the possibility of earning a great deal of money impressed him. If it did he gave no sign. Instead he asked, 'How long have you been involved in this sort of work?'

'With the company, over five years. In this particular field, almost a year.' She answered automatically, half her mind still mulling the fact that he appeared to have no interest in the rewards the operation would bring to him. That worried her a little. In her experience, love of money was the most powerful motivator. It was a trait she understood and could handle, but if the trait wasn't there she might find herself hard-pressed to deal with it, to cope with his actions.

As Karen considered all the possibilities, Richard turned back to the map, apparently lost in thought as he turned it around in his hand. After a few moments he asked quietly, 'Have you ever been involved with something as dangerous as this before? It'll be a tough assignment, even for a man, and five years seems a very short time to give you so much responsibility.' He gave her a grin, his stance challenging, 'I mean, you seem a little on the young side for something like this.'

She took up the challenge, her impatience well under control. 'I'm twenty five if that's what you're fishing to know. And don't worry,

I've handled similar things before—you've no need to worry about my lack of experience.'

Richard looked at her with those startling dark eyes of his, still grinning a little. 'A good age for a woman, old enough to have learned something about herself—and the world.'

He laughed easily and turned back to the map. For a while he said nothing but his face had taken on a more serious expression. 'I suppose you've considered all the difficulties?' he said quietly at last. 'The world's full of people who'd stoop to anything with this amount of money involved.'

'I know that there is a certain element that would do just about anything to beat us to the gold coins.'

Richard looked at her cryptically. 'Actually, you could be quite wrong about that.' He saw her puzzled look and explained, 'If anyone else knows about it, all they have to do is sit back and let us do all the spade work. When it's found, they'll make their move.'

'We've already thought of that,' she admitted, 'but it makes no difference, we'll have to go ahead. We must make sure that our security is water-tight from the start. No leaks.'

'How many people in London know what you're here for?'

'Only my immediate boss, Sir James.'

'Did you make your own arrangements to come here, or have you a secretary to do that kind of thing for you?'

'Our travel department did that.'

'So that's at least one other person, the clerk in the travel office.'

'But she only arranged the car and my expenses. I booked the ferry myself.'

'Where's your car now?'

'On the mainland, at the harbour. I couldn't see any point in bringing it across here.'

'So, there's the fleet car people, the harbour board, and anyone else who may have seen you.'

'Yes,' her tone was a little stiff, 'but I don't believe that any of those people could have known what my real reason was for coming here. It's quite normal for me to visit prospective leisure areas; it's part of my job as an insurance assessor, so it's perfectly reasonable for me to check it out.'

'And suppose I refuse to have you along?'

Karen smiled gently. 'It's very simple, Mr Marshall. I've shown you the wrong map.'

Richard let loose with a string of blistering curses, then regaining some semblance of composure asked, 'So, where's the real one?'

'You don't believe I'd walk around with something like that in my pocket, do you?' She held his challenge full on. 'I've committed most of what we need to know to memory and left the hard proof in the safe at the office. Everything I've told you is the truth and the coins are definitely here, but only I and my boss knows precisely where to look.'

'You've got it all worked out haven't you?'

'Yes. And if you refuse to have me along, then we have no choice but to get someone else—we can do that, you know—there are ways of getting around everything, including your ownership of the islands.'

She saw his eyes narrow dangerously. 'Are you making some kind of threat?'

'I'm merely letting you know that we can get over any problems if you refuse your cooperation.'

She waited for Richard's response, and as she watched his changing expressions she could see that he was sorely tempted to tell her to find someone else.

She waited patiently until he finally muttered, 'You'll have to do your share of work. I don't carry passengers.'

'Agreed,' Karen responded readily. 'How soon can you get things started?'

'We will need to talk more about the location.'

'That's no problem—I can draw out a rough sketch.'

'Then it shouldn't take long. You probably noticed that the island is rocky so we may even need to organise climbing as well as diving gear. The north side is craggy, nothing but caves, so we'll have to use the boat.'

She nodded. 'Would that be a problem?'

'Not at all, I already own one.'

'How long will it take to get ready?'

27

'She's always ready. But we may need more equipment than we have on the island, such as oxygen masks . . .'

'Oxygen masks?'

Richard shot her an amused look. 'If we have to go into any of the caves we'll have to enter them by sea. We'll probably have to swim under the rocks to reach some of the entrances. It's doubtful even you could hold your breath for that long.'

Karen deliberately ignored his mockery. 'Can we get everything we need from the mainland?'

'Not all at once. If you want to keep this operation a secret we'll have to pick up the pieces a little at a time from different places. We'll have to give the impression that you've hired me for a short cruise. It'll take longer, but it'll be safer in the long run.'

'If you say so,' Karen murmured. She knew she would have to defer to him on some things if only to keep him agreeable.

They spent the remainder of the morning discussing equipment, and any likely problems that they may meet. In the afternoon, after a working lunch, Richard took her down to the harbour where his boat lay at anchor.

The *Bonny Bride* looked deceptively small from the harbour wall, but when she was aboard Karen conceded that it was beautiful. Below deck Richard showed her into a spaciously comfortable cabin and informed her that it was to be hers while they were at sea. It was compact, and bigger than she would have imagined. It could easily sleep six or seven.

After endless discussion they had dinner together, and a little after ten o'clock she sank into bed in the pretty bedroom above the terraced rose-garden.

She awoke at dawn, showered then dressed, deciding on jeans and a sleeveless cotton top as the most sensible rigout for a day afloat.

A man was sitting in the breakfast room and he looked up in surprise as Karen entered. He rose to his feet and gave her a vaguely familiar crooked grin, and she knew she wasn't dreaming, 'Hello, Karen,' he said.

'Mike! What in Heaven's name are you doing here?'

'I work here.'

She shook her head in bewildered surprise. This was too much of a coincidence to accept. 'Since when?'

'Since I left Launceston and Broome. I was just making myself some coffee. Want some?'

Recoiling a little from her surprise at seeing an old colleague so casually making coffee in the kitchen at Gwyn Radyr Fawr, Karen sat down, and asked, 'What on earth made you come all the way down here?'

Mike turned his head and grinned, switching on the percolator. 'Long story,' he replied.

She didn't know Mike Johnson very well,

although she'd seen him around for a long time. She remembered he'd been an investigator with her company long before she began her climb up the ladder, and she'd bumped into him many times around the office.

She'd heard along the grapevine that he'd given up his job fairly abruptly and she'd no idea why he had, but to suddenly find him here at Gwyn Radyr Fawr was incredible. 'Whatever made you give up your job to come out here?'

'In a nutshell, I wanted to work with boats.'

She gave a small shrug. 'Well, you've come to the right place for that I suppose, but it's quite a switch, isn't it? There's no comparison to the work you've been trained for.'

Mike shrugged. 'It is a bit.' He broke off a corner of his toast and popped it into his mouth. 'I've always loved sailing and there's plenty of that here. Last year, when I heard they needed a crewman for the Round Britain race—I jumped at it. I've been here ever since.'

'I would never have thought you to be the outdoor type, Mike.'

He grinned over the rim of his coffee cup. 'Neither did I, but I felt it was time I opted out of the rat race.' Then he grinned more widely, sizing her up. 'I heard he was expecting someone from London to look over the island, but I never thought in a million years it would be you. I thought you'd have been married by

30

now.'

'Not yet.'

'But what's it all about? Why have they sent someone as senior as you? Lovell usually handles the insurance for land conversions.'

She saw no reason to rid him of the notion that she was here merely to look over the island. 'I was available. Anyway, what makes you think I'm working? This is a beautiful place. Maybe I just came down here for a holiday.'

'Where are you off to now?'

'Around the island,' she smiled brightly, 'just taking things as they come.'

He clearly didn't believe her, but Karen wasn't going to waste time worrying about it. She smiled again, tossed back the remainder of her coffee, then left the room.

Richard was already waiting for her in the drive when she went out. The back of the car was crammed with gear and tins of food in cardboard boxes. He was wearing the same casual denims and sandals that he had worn the day before, and he still hadn't bothered to shave. When he saw her he scowled, 'What's taken you so long? I wanted to get an early start.'

'And a pleasant day to you, too,' she said shortly as she stepped into the car. 'Are you always so charming in the mornings?'

He shrugged broad, bare shoulders then started up the car, turning it towards the

31

harbour. 'When we get on board you can start by stowing that stuff away into the galley,' he nodded his head to the back seat, 'and then you can help me with the charts.'

'Seeing Mike Johnson working here has given me a bit of a surprise,' she remarked once they were away from the house and on their way to the harbour. 'I've just been talking to him in the kitchen.'

Richard turned quickly, a bright gleam of astonishment lighting his dark eyes. 'I didn't know you knew him.'

Karen nodded her head. her tawny hair looking even more afire with the brightness of the sun. 'He was a colleague of mine once.'

He didn't say any more. He shifted his grip on the wheel, keeping his eyes fastened on the twisting narrow road ahead. Karen stole a glance at his profile, seeing in his expression something more than surprise. There was a cold little twist to his mouth and she sensed that her knowledge of Mike had had quite an effect on him.

The sun was well risen above the horizon and the day was already hot as they went on board the boat. Karen smiled when she spotted the boat's name painted boldly along its side, *Bonny Bride*. 'Unusual name,' she commented, 'does it have some mysterious cryptic meaning?'

'There's nothing mysterious about my boat. She's my one true love. The only bride I'll ever want.' Richard grinned, catching her smile.

She gave a little snort. 'I suppose that's because she's putty in your hands? Never answers you back?'

Richard's strong arms heaved the provisions on board as though they were made of paper. He glanced up at her question with a smile. 'That's part of it. Bride's always been a popular lady around here.'

She looked at him in surprise, 'So there is a lady called Bride on Gwyn Radyr Fawr?'

He tossed back his head and laughed, his teeth gleaming whitely against his tanned face. 'Only in spirit, the original's been dead for centuries.'

'So tell me who was this popular lady who's been so honoured by your giving her name to your boat?'

'She was Brigantic. Bride's just another form of it. She became St Bride because the early Christians placed her as the midwife to the Virgin, but the Welsh know her better as one of their favourite sea-goddesses. Dozens of wells are named after her—you've probably come across one or two—and because she lived in the water, she's supposed to be very fond of sailors and sea creatures and . . .' His pause made Karen look up to find him grinning at her, '. . . and, like me . . .' he went on provokingly, '. . . she hates women.'

'Oh, really.' Karen responded dismissively.

Between them they stowed away the cans of

food, bread, fruit, and even, Karen spotted, a case of wine.

'We'll make for St David's Bay first. We can take on a couple of oxygen bottles there and another wet suit, then we'll go a little further up the coast to a place I know beyond Fishguard.'

'Are you sure all this cloak-and-dagger stuff is really necessary?' Karen asked as she struggled to tie back a heavy unwieldy rope which was part of the rigging.

'I am. And watch what you're doing with that rope.'

'I'm not exactly Popeye you know,' she snapped. 'Anyway, I think you should be doing this kind of thing yourself and leave me to the galley and the charting.'

Her arms were aching, and she could feel the sun already burning her skin through the sun-tan lotion. The wind was whipping her hair across her face so that she could hardly see. On top of everything else she was hungry, having skipped breakfast.

'I told you this operation wouldn't be easy,' he pointed out smugly.

Karen straightened and glared at him. Something about this man brought out the worst in her. Angrily she snapped, 'I don't expect it to be easy, and I'll do my share, don't worry about that. Now, unless there's anything else, I'm going below.'

Without waiting for his response, she

stomped down the gangway leading to the galley below deck.

'Make some breakfast while you're there,' Richard yelled after her. 'That is, if you know how to cook.'

Below, as Karen found space in the cramped cupboards for the food, she reasoned that she was going to be stuck with Richard Marshall for weeks; there was no point in crossing swords with each other all the time. So, just over half an hour later she carried two plates on deck and set up a small folding table, positioning it by the cabin.

'Not bad for a beginner,' he said after he had polished off six rashers of bacon, three eggs and a mountain of toast. 'Your coffee's not too bad, either.'

'Thank you,' Karen murmured. 'I'm pleased my humble efforts meet with your gracious approval.'

He grinned slowly. 'Perhaps I was a little hard on you just then. But you have to admit it took a lot of nerve bringing you along. A woman's bad news on a sailing yacht. They're unlucky.' She decided to try to ignore such comments from now on.

'About other people being interested in this operation . . . did you really mean it?'

Richard refilled their cups before he answered.

His voice had taken on a low, pensive tone. 'In some ways nothing ever changes. People

35

are people no matter what century it is. Greed is greed, whether it's a crew of old-time sailors press-ganged for a medieval king hell-bent on a crown, or just a plain, modern, everyday crook who wants to get rich quick. It can get very dangerous.'

'If you're trying to put me off, you're succeeding.'

Richard laughed. 'I doubt that! You don't strike me as the type who could scare easily.' Then his voice softened a little. 'I'm not trying to put you off. All I'm trying to do is to warn you that it could get rough.'

Something in his tone made her stomach turn. She hadn't bargained on any trouble and Sir James certainly hadn't warned her of any. Normally she was a fairly good sailor, but suddenly her breakfast wasn't sitting lightly.

He caught her look. 'Don't worry, I'm hoping it'll appear like you've hired me to take you for an innocent boat trip. That should throw anybody off the track.'

'Is that how you see us?'

'It's the safest bet, and anyway, having a girl on board could be good camouflage.'

'I see,' she replied stiffly, very aware of the implication.

'There's no need to get on your high horse again. You know exactly what I mean. We could give the impression that we want to be together.' Their eyes met as he added, 'Could you manage that?'

'I might have to work at it.'

Karen stood up quickly, wary of her thoughts going along the wrong tracks again, and started to clear away the breakfast things. 'What do you want me to do when I'm finished with these?'

Richard stood up as well and swung lithely back to the rigging to get the *Bonny Bride* under way again. 'Nothing for now,' his voice sounding muffled in the heavy canvas of the rigging. 'You can get some practice in at being a tourist and I'll call you if I need you.'

Below deck, as she rinsed the dishes, she suddenly thought of Malcolm. Her face flushed guiltily as she thought of him. Why did she suddenly feel this way? She put up a hand to her cheek—why on earth was she suddenly so pricked with guilt? She'd done nothing to bring on this feeling, had she? But deep down inside, she knew exactly why she was feeling like she was. She hadn't given her fiancé a single thought in almost two days—nor had she been in touch. Malcolm would be furious!

She decided to write to him tonight, to ease her conscience a little. Better still, she would telephone him as soon as she reached shore. Once she'd spoken to him everything would fall back neatly into place.

CHAPTER THREE

The next morning, after Karen had breakfasted and had given Malcolm's letter to Mrs Williams to post, they set off on *Bonny Bride* for the pin-point of high-cliffed islet that lay some 20 miles west of the island of Gwyn Radyr Fawr.

From her vantage point at the porthole, Karen watched the tiny mooring grow smaller and smaller as *Bonny Bride* moved away from the shore. The sea was calm and clear and the wind was fresh, filling the sails. It wouldn't be very long before they rounded the headland towards their destination.

She could hear Richard moving about on deck and considered going up to help, but decided against it. She knew that she was really more of a hindrance than a help, and besides, she had a feeling that Richard wanted to be alone for a while.

If the location was correct, they should reach it within a couple of hours, and then neither of them would get much rest. She needed time to think; time to consider what steps she would have to take if the money was recovered, and the best way to get it to London.

She spent the next two hours in her cabin, poring over the more promising locations around the island. On deck, Richard navigated the yacht into a narrow channel between the towering cliffs. Once free of the dangerous rocks lying just below the surface, he anchored *Bonny Bride* in the still waters of the natural harbour.

From below deck, Karen could hear him moving about, setting both the stern and the bow anchors, as well as running out a line to the shore and tying it to a sharp crevice where the rocks had been split open by the crashing waves. She watched from the porthole and was impressed by his foresight. It was unlikely they would be seen, but, apart from the line giving them more stability, it meant that if they had to get away quickly, it could be cut from the deck.

It was early in the afternoon when Karen went on deck. Richard lounged in an old deck-chair, his long legs stretched out in front of him, and the deep shadow of the cliffs obscuring any expression. She looked around, admiring the spectacular scenery.

'What a lovely spot. I'd like to come back here some day,' she murmured, 'when I have time to appreciate it properly.'

He grinned. 'You could be my first official tourist.'

'I'd think I'd prefer that. This operation could get a bit scary.' She smiled, somewhat sheepishly.

'It goes with the job. You'll get used to it.'

She gave a shaky laugh. 'I'm counting on you to see we both come out of this on the winning side.'

He regarded her sombrely. He was looking at her in a strange way and it disconcerted her. 'You may be counting on too much,' he mumbled at last, 'I'm only human.'

She didn't need him to tell her that. He was vital and virile, and everything about him made her acutely aware of her femininity. The irony of their situation did not escape her. They were in one of the most idyllic spots on earth, not a soul within miles: unwilling partners, wary of themselves and each other.

'Do you think anyone knows we're here?' Karen asked, breaking the tense silence that had fallen between them.

'If there is, they'll keep well out of sight.'

Richard gave her a dry smile. 'Cheer up, it's unlikely that anyone's here. Besides, we have other things to worry about.'

'Such as?'

'We could have a storm, or an engine breakdown, or both. Or we could be in entirely the wrong place and it will all have been a complete waste of time.'

'I really appreciate your optimism,' Karen muttered.

Richard laughed, 'Well, I wouldn't want you to get bored by the whole thing being too easy.'

'We should be so lucky,' she said under her

breath.

'To be on the safe side, we'll have a training run this afternoon.'

Karen looked up quickly, but said nothing.

'You don't know these rocks. I'll need to go down with you a couple of times until I feel you'll be safe alone.'

She didn't question him. He was right. She felt no need for him to spell out that if something happened, if she should injure herself, or worse, if he should injure himself helping her out of difficulties, she would have no way of handling the situation alone.

Over coffee they discussed the location where the treasure was believed to lie.

'Let's hope we can get in and out quickly.' Karen found herself wishing that she could feel a little more confident about diving into such dangerous waters. Rugged pinnacles of rock projected out of the swirling foam, and the jagged, overhanging cliffs seemed to threaten any intrusion into this wild place.

'Don't be too optimistic about finding Henry Tudor's pennies. According to the sonar there's nothing at all down there.'

She gestured to the diagram. 'But there must be . . .'

'On the other hand,' he added, 'it could be lying at an angle and blocked by debris. A lot of ships went down off these rocks in the old days. But, if it's there, we'll find it.'

They pored over the likely sites, and then

41

Richard instructed her how to take a compass bearing and how to sound the depth. She found herself becoming more familiar with the rigging and the winches, and Richard gave her a crash test at the radio in case that avenue of escape should be needed.

What she did find remarkable during those few hectic hours was the beauty of the boat, and a deep understanding of Richard's love of it. She felt she knew now why he had chosen to live the life he had. The boat was a world in itself, where the only reality was the sea and the wind, and when this job came to an end, and it was time for her to leave, she knew she would feel some regrets.

Richard checked that *Bonny Bride* was secure, making sure that both the forward and aft anchors were in their place, then they prepared to submerge.

Karen struggled into her wet-suit and Richard helped her on with her equipment, then he moved behind her to secure the air tanks into place.

She sagged a little under their weight and gripped the straps tightly. 'They're heavier than I remember.'

He slipped his own tanks into place as though the weight was negligible to him. 'These tanks hold an hour's supply. We shouldn't need it all, but I'd rather be safe than sorry.'

After a final check on their equipment, they

climbed down the metal ladder at the stern and lowered themselves into the water. Karen put her mouthpiece into place. She concentrated on her breathing for several seconds, remembering not to inhale through her nose, getting the hang of it quickly enough. After a few moments, Richard slid into the water with Karen following close behind him.

She followed Richard through the glittering rainbow of effervescent air-bubbles which escaped in luminous spirals from his mask, and entered a world of enchantment. The water so pure that every detail around her stood out clear and sharp. She was enthralled by the huge colourful boulders and crags, shelving deeply and festooned with all manner of seaweeds and marine plants. Here and there she caught the gleam of an inquisitive fish, but the fish were shy and darted away like bright streaks of lightning at the intrusion of these bold strangers from another world.

She had only a few moments to take in the breathtaking beauty of this undersea world before Richard flashed a powerful beam of his torch, indicating an arched gap in the wall of the rocks. He motioned her to follow him and they swam downwards at a steep angle. In theory, she thought she knew where she was, but in reality she felt disorientated and doubted her own navigation.

Karen followed Richard through the tortuously narrow gap, keeping directly behind

43

him. The water darkened as they swam deeper. For several minutes she could see nothing through the murky darkness, then abruptly Richard pointed with his torch to the entrance of an underwater cave.

As they swam closer to it, Karen could see then that there was more than one, each as dark and forbidding as the next. They slowed their pace as Richard examined each one in turn, testing their width with his body and assessing the least dangerous possibility of entry.

After a few moments he swam up to her side, slipping an arm around her wet-suited waist, and indicating with a lift of his head that it was time to go back. They turned and retraced their manoeuvrings through the gap and swam upwards towards the sunlight.

He grabbed hold of her hand as they climbed on board, pulling her on to the deck of *Bonny Bride*, and without speaking a word, they removed their equipment, neither of them admitting yet that the caves looked as though they would prove difficult to enter.

Richard stood slightly bent over with his hands on his knees, breathing deeply. Salty seawater dripped off him in long rivulets, flowing down his tanned chest and limbs and to distract herself, Karen briskly dried herself off. 'Well, what do you think?' she asked. 'Is it an impossibility?'

Richard didn't answer at once and when he

caught her glance, he said distractedly, 'It's worse than I thought. I'll have to go down again to find the best way of entry.'

'But it *is* possible, isn't it?'

He gave a restrained laugh and nodded his dark head. 'All things are possible. Don't worry, we'll find a way.'

The light was rapidly fading, and they were both so tired that they agreed to postpone any further work until next day. Karen made supper and after they had eaten she said goodnight and went below.

She changed into a cotton slip, too tired to do anything more with the maps tonight. She curled up on the bunk and eased her tired legs along its cool cotton duvet.

She was soon in a dreamlike state, trying to fall asleep, but slipping in and out of wakefulness.

The soft tap on her door was so gentle that she wasn't sure whether she had heard it or not.

Again she heard the tapping, and this time, Richard's voice, 'Are you sleep?'

'No. Come in, the door's not locked.'

The door opened and Karen smiled as she saw Richard standing there balancing two glasses of wine in one hand. 'Fancy a nightcap?'

'Just for a few minutes, then I must get some sleep.'

He set her wine glass on the cabinet by her

side and sat down. He sat very still for a few moments then he raised his glass to his lips, 'Here's to success,' he smiled, taking a sip.

Those hypnotic eyes bored into her own, making it impossible to shift her gaze. He ran a caressing finger along her bare arm. 'Your skin is soft—like silk,' he said huskily. 'It seemed a pity to cover it in a wet-suit today.'

She laughed jerkily, 'Soft skin or not, I would have frozen to death without it.'

His eyes moved over her. With a hint of reproach in her tone, she murmured, 'Richard, you've only come in here for a nightcap, remember?'

'Of course—I'm a man of integrity!' His smile broke into a devilish grin.

'That's what they all say.'

He straightened up. 'You're right, of course. We would be playing with fire and I'm not going to risk it . . .' He gave a small sigh and after a moment admitted softly and unexpectedly, 'The trouble is, you must know how attractive you are, Karen. And I'm only a man. A man who feels strongly attracted to you And who knows that deep down you feel the same about me. You can't deny it, can you?'

Karen didn't move or speak. There was no denying the obvious.

He stood up. 'Trust me to get landed with someone like you,' he said morosely. 'Why couldn't they have sent Lovell? Avoided complications . . .'

Karen turned away, averting her eyes.

'I'm tired, Richard,' she insisted gently. 'Let's get some sleep, it's only a few hours to dawn.'

He stood a moment longer. His dark eyes filled with thoughts and emotions she could not read, or perhaps was afraid to.

When he'd gone, she closed her eyes, willing sleep, but it wouldn't come. To think that she'd always believed herself to be in control of her life. What a joke!

There was something about Richard's wild, untamed masculinity that beckoned her, attracted her despite all her misgivings. Perhaps in another place, another time . . .

At last, a disturbed sleep overtook her. Images of dark, forbidding caves lying inaccessibly below, fathoms deep, interspersed with vague images of Richard . . .

CHAPTER FOUR

The clock was a signal for a return to a heavy stillness. She lay there for some time thinking over Richard's effect on her from the night before.

Something had to be done. She couldn't carry on like this. They had a job to do and her attraction to Richard was beginning to overcome everything else. She must put a stop to it and get back to concentrating on her work and the unassailable fact that she was still engaged to Malcolm.

With a sigh, Karen got up, dressed and went up on deck to find Richard already at work in the wheelhouse. He was adjusting one of the instruments on the panel, and when she entered he didn't smile. In fact, he showed no emotion of any kind, but tension flowed out of him like an electric current.

Karen sensed his mood immediately. Looking directly into his eyes she said, 'Richard, I think we'd better talk.'

He jerked his head to one side, looking at her warily, but his voice when he replied was full of approval. 'That makes sense. Where shall we start?'

He swung himself on to the seat, his tension easing and his eyes mocking as he waited for her to continue. 'Well . . . ? I'm listening.'

Gathering up her courage she went on hastily, 'I know what you're thinking . . .'

'You do?'

Her hair gleamed in the morning sun and the light in her emerald eyes glittered with determination. 'Look, Richard, we'll soon have this job finished and then we'll go our separate ways. I—I don't want either of us to get hurt.'

A deep sigh escaped him. He leaned back against the partition and closed his eyes, opening them a moment later to find her peering at him anxiously. His mouth quirked upwards into a smile. 'I admire your honesty, Karen, but has it occurred to you that this isn't the best time to care for somebody, anyway.'

'You mean because of the danger we might run into?'

He nodded. 'That, and the fact that neither of us wants to change anything in our lives.'

They met each other's eyes, holding each other in challenge, then Richard smiled. He turned back to the instrument panel, leaving Karen in no doubt that the discussion was closed as far as he was concerned.

Later, as they were having breakfast, two helicopters flew overhead, and Richard followed their movements with narrowed eyes.

'Do you recognise them?' Karen asked. 'Can you make out the markings?'

He shook his head. ' 'Fraid not, they could be anybody.'

Karen watched him for a moment, then asked quietly, 'Do you think we're under surveillance?'

'I don t know.' Then he turned and gave her a quick grin. 'It could be Sir James checking on his investment.'

'I don't like it,' Karen protested, her eyes squinting in the sunlight as she watched the helicopters make another circuit above them, dip low and then fade away in the distance.

'It's no use looking for trouble. It's probably someone out on a training flight; there's a flying school over by Bryn Garw. You're just getting a bit jumpy. Come on, help me get fitted out, I want to get started.'

Her eyes widened in surprise. 'What do you mean, get started? You're surely not going down alone?'

'Yes, I am. Last night after I left you I did a lot of thinking. I had a lot on my mind, not least of which was the best and safest way to get into that damned cave, and I think I've found one.'

'I'll come with you . . .'

'No, you stay here and look after things on board. I'll be better on my own—you must stay here and feed me the line.'

'What line?'

'The marker line,' he said patiently, pointing to a coil of rope by the capstan. 'We'll be quicker using a line.'

Karen felt apprehensive. 'But anything

could happen to you down there.'

'Just keep concentrating on what I tell you to do. I'll go down and mark out the best way in,' he instructed, moving towards the rail and hauling the oxygen cylinders on his back.

He reached the rail of the deck and prepared to enter the water. 'Keep feeding that guide rope out to me and when I find the best way in I'll give two jerks to tell you to mark the rope and tie it. Then I'll give three more when it's time to reel it in. If anything should happen, just give one almighty tug and I'll be back right away. Is that clear?'

Reluctantly Karen nodded her head. He readjusted his equipment, and then with a movement swift and effortless, he flipped over into the water. She watched his reflection as he dived, but within seconds not a ripple was left to show where he had gone.

Karen fed the line out slowly. It seemed ages before she felt the two strong jerks on the other end, but glancing at her watch she saw that only 15 minutes had passed since he'd entered the water.

She marked the rope with daubs of black paint and tied it fast to the capstan. Reaching for a rag to wipe her hands she saw a gleam of light and she looked up to see what it was. A large motorlaunch was lying at anchor about half a mile from *Bonny Bride*, but at that distance she couldn't recognise it. Squinting her eyes, their silhouettes blurred against the deck lights, she could just about make out the shape of three people. They were clustered together at the helm, and whoever they were they certainly seemed interested in *Bonny Bride*.

With a worried frown she turned her attention back to the job in hand. It was probably nothing. Perhaps it was a party of men out for a day's fishing. After all, she told herself, it was a common enough sight around these waters. Reaching for the binoculars, she kept her eyes glued to the newcomers. They seemed innocent enough so she was probably over-reacting again.

A little while later she saw two of the men in skin-diving gear slip into the water. Suddenly she was afraid and wished Richard would hurry up. The fact that these men were diving so close was stretching coincidence a little too far.

Her hands gripped the rope and she pulled at it, giving a tug that took almost all her strength. She waited nervously for Richard's answering tug and it wasn't long before it came.

As Richard broke the water on *Bonny Bride*'s port side, Karen was already hauling up the marker rope. He swung himself up on to the deck as she wound the last of it around the capstan and throwing Richard a nervous glance, she breathed, 'We've got company.'

Turning, Richard caught sight of the other

boat. He studied the elegant lines of the blue and red hull as Karen explained what she had seen.

'They looked like they knew what they were after,' she told him, referring to the other divers. 'And I don't think it's a very good idea that you should stay down while they're around.'

'You're probably right,' he said gruffly, 'I'd like to know more about what they're up to.'

She nodded, 'What do we do now?'

He laid a hand on her arm and hesitated a moment before saying quietly, 'Nothing for the moment. I'll go down again after it's gone dark. I think I've found the entrance, so tomorrow morning we'll radio Sir James to tell him we've found the area, but drawn a blank on the coins.'

'Why tell him that when we don't know yet?'

'Just in case our friends over there are listening in—it'll throw them off.'

Karen didn't agree with his plan at all. For him to go down again after dark was too dangerous to contemplate. She would rather have gone alongside the other boat, and on the pretext of being on just a friendly holiday cruise, tried to find out more about these people. She said as much to Richard.

'You're not in the polite world of the boardroom now. You don't understand this situation. Anything could happen in the next five minutes, let alone the next couple of days.'

On that optimistic note he went below, and she heard him whistling as he changed his clothes as if he hadn't a care in the world.

Frowning, Karen finished securing the marker rope, then mopped the pools of water from the deck where Richard had been standing. At least it was something to do, and it occupied her trembling hands.

Keeping her head down, she lifted her eyes towards the other boat. It was still at anchor and she could see that there were again three figures moving about the deck—the two divers had come back on board. All three men were looking towards *Bonny Bride*, and Karen continued to go through the motions of deck-swabbing for a few minutes more before going down below to join Richard.

She found him seated at the table towelling his hair. He had changed into shorts and a tee-shirt and Karen allowed her eyes to move over him for a moment before she said, 'They're still there. Do you think they'll do anything?'

'Not as long as we're out of the water,' he replied, his voice muffled by the towel. He threw it down into a basket and went on, 'They could be just innocent people out on a pleasure dive, and perhaps a little curious about us. If they're not, then as long as we stay on board they'll think we haven't found anything yet and leave us alone until we do.'

Karen nodded and, despite everything. she giggled. He looked at her quizzically, 'What's

54

so funny?'

'Your hair,' she admitted, 'it looks as though you've had an electric shock. It's all over the place.' His dark tangled curls were sticking out in all directions, giving him a wild, untamed look.

Richard grinned wryly, 'It needs cutting.'

He stretched his long legs out in front of him, looking at her quizzically.

'Now tell me something about yourself.'

Karen turned away. She hated talking about the past. It unsettled her. All her life she had tried to find something that would keep her satisfied, fulfilled, but she never had. Always there was an ache—a longing for *something*, she didn't know what—and it ate away at her.

In spite of her well-paid job, her success, and her elegant mews apartment in London, she would have given it all up gladly to feel as though she belonged to someone—something. Even Malcolm had failed to stifle it yet, but maybe when they had children . . .

Richard's gaze had not left her for a moment and a small kernel of pride knotted inside her. 'Don't feel sorry for me,' she said coldly, recognising his expression, 'I've made a success of my life and I'll carry on doing so. I don't need anyone except myself.'

'Are you quite sure about that?' he asked, standing up and pulling the towel from his shoulders.

Karen held his gaze. His mouth was formed

into a vague approximation of a smile, but it was a gentle smile. As was the hand that reached out and stroked her cheek. She stiffened slightly at his touch, but only for an instant.

He waited, giving her the chance to say something. Karen knew that whatever she decided, he would accept it. He had taken the first step. His eyes told her everything; they told her that he was vulnerable, but whatever she said, he would accept.

It was his eyes that told her he would be hurt by her rejection, that he cared enough to be hurt. And she knew she felt the same. But in spite of her feelings she knew it could only be temporary, and she must never lose sight of the fact.

Fate seemed to be playing a joke on her. She would hurt too much when this was over. She and Richard came from entirely different worlds, and somehow she felt that, to him at least, women were a pleasant diversion. Interludes to be enjoyed like a warm summer night, or good wine . . .

She didn't want to be in love with Richard Marshall. She didn't want to commit herself forever to this man who could promise her nothing.

She broke away suddenly.

'Why are you so afraid?' Richard said quietly. 'There is something between us—a moment in our lives that we could both enjoy . . .'

'I'm not afraid,' she replied, her voice little more than a whisper.

'Then what's wrong?' His tone was soft and pleading, but Karen didn't answer—she couldn't trust herself to speak.

Richard took a step back, his eyes like black coals. 'I won't lie to you, Karen.' His words sounded like chips of ice. 'There are times when I want you very much.' He brought his eyes down sharply to her face. 'I know I shouldn't speak like this, it's just that I—' He left the sentence unfinished as he plunged through the door into his cabin.

CHAPTER FIVE

There was no sound from Richard's cabin for the next half-hour, and after a while Karen went up on deck. The new moon was already shining whitely through the thin clouds, and a gentle wind blew from the west.

She leaned over the rails, watching the still water lap gently around the sides of the boat. It was quiet. Looking out across the water to the launch as it lay at anchor, the moon's rays caught its brass trimmings, causing them to glimmer intermittently like candles on a cake. There was no movement. The men on board must be asleep now.

Karen sat herself down on the capstan and cupped her face in her hands, trying desperately to concentrate her thoughts on Malcolm. But his face wouldn't come into her mind, no matter how hard she tried. Her stomach twisted painfully. Her throat was tight and, despite the warm night, her hand felt cold and clammy against her cheeks.

Sitting there, with only a cabin's door separating her from Richard Marshall, Karen thought over her situation. Apart from the terrible dejection and frustration, there was something else troubling her. She had abandoned her one golden rule. Self-sufficiency. She had allowed herself to care—

to care very much . . .

She turned quickly at the sound of movement behind her. It was Richard. In the fading daylight Karen saw that he was already dressed in his wet-suit.

At her quizzical look, he shrugged. 'I couldn't sleep.' He lowered himself on to the capstan beside her, resting his arms on his knees and said, 'No point in worrying about things.'

She sighed and rested her head against the wheelhouse. 'No point at all, but I can't help it.'

'Are you nervous about me going down in the dark?'

'Yes, I am.'

He turned his head to look at her. 'Are you afraid of what might happen?'

He put his arm around her shoulder and drew her against him. She rested her head on his shoulder and he settled more comfortably. They stayed like that for a little while then he stirred. 'What are you thinking about?'

His voice at her side pulled her out of her reverie and she turned towards him with a slow smile. 'Nothing.'

'I'll give you a penny for them.' Richard looked at her for a moment, his eyes thoughtful, then he broke into that broad smile which was becoming so familiar to her now, and it never failed to stop her heart—it seemed to lighten his whole expression. He lifted up her hand, his fingers twisting the intricate diamond ring. 'Are you thinking about your fiancé?'

She sat up abruptly and looked at him darkly. 'That's not fair.'

Richard was surprised by the quick anger that had suddenly flashed into her eyes, and he held up his hands in a gesture of mock surrender. 'Don't get so mad, I'm only curious.'

'Why did you have to bring Malcolm up?'

'I'm sorry,' Richard said softly. 'Let's forget it, shall we?'

'Yes, let's.'

She sat back and examined Richard's grim expression as he studied her. He gave an odd little twisted smile then said quietly, 'Did I touch a nerve then? I didn't mean to.'

'It's just that I don't want to talk about my private life,' Karen answered evenly.

Richard nodded. 'I can see that.' A moody darkness crept into his expression and his eyes deepened. 'I'd better make a move.' He got up and reached for the air bottle. 'The same signals as before, OK?'

She nodded and helped him on with the air bottle. 'Have you got the torch?' she asked.

He gestured to the underwater light tied around his waist. It would be his only illumination when he entered the water. As he climbed down the steps, the tanks on his back glinted darkly in the pale light of the moon, and he entered the water with barely a splash. He gave Karen a quick thumbs-up signal, then he was gone.

The rope gave out without a sound as she fed it out. Richard had made sure that it had been well oiled earlier, but even so, Karen was tense with nervous apprehension. It was all too easy to imagine what it must be like to be diving through the impenetrable blackness below with only the single beam of a torch to guide the way.

She waited for what seemed an endless time until he tugged again. He'd reached the gap and that was the signal for her to feed more line as he went through. This was the worst part, because there was nothing Karen could do then until he was back on board, hopefully with a safe route through the caves.

At long last, three tugs came through. He'd made it! With shaking hands, she began to reel the rope in, reeling very slowly to avoid making any sound, and soon Richard was surfacing and lifting himself out of the water.

'There is a way,' he whispered, the excitement evident in his voice. 'With a bit of luck we'll both go down tomorrow. Any trouble up here?'

'No, nothing. I think they're all still asleep.'

'Good. Let's hope we're wrong about them.'

He stripped off and went below. Karen followed. The galley portholes were blacked out by heavy curtains, and she sat down on the bunk seat by the door. Richard looked tired as he seated himself at the table and drew a sketch of the route through the gap.

'There's an old wreck lying right across it but I've found a way through,' he said, throwing her a quick glance. 'We could have it all wrapped tomorrow if it wasn't for our uninvited company. We'll try to throw them off and have another go in a couple of days. After that, Sir James can handle it.'

Karen inhaled slowly. 'Then our job will be finished and all that remains is for my company to hand over the fat cheque you've earned.'

He didn't look up, and for a few moments neither of them spoke. Then Richard murmured, 'That doesn't mean much except for the freedom it'll bring.'

She studied him closely as he opened one of the drawers in the table and threw the rough drawing in. Did freedom mean so much to him then? It sounded like it. She thrust the thought aside and tried to concentrate on more immediate matters. 'We still have tomorrow to get through.'

'I haven't forgotten. Let's call it a day, and at first light tomorrow well see how the land lies with our friends over there.'

Without another word he got up and went into his cabin to get some rest. For a while Karen sat alone in the galley, thinking over all that had happened.

Later, lying on her bunk, she stared at the ceiling and tried not to think about Richard. She fell asleep, waking up shortly after daybreak to find him already on deck as usual.

There was no movement from the other boat as Richard and Karen drank their early morning coffee in almost total silence. It was broken only by the most perfunctory remarks about the weather and the job which lay before them. Afterwards, at Richard's suggestion, Karen put a call through to Sir James, relaying the story they had agreed on.

'It doesn't look as though there's anything here, Sir James,' she began. 'We seem to have located the spot but it looks as though we could have been wrong about the *Tudor Warrior*.'

'That's most disappointing . . .' Sir James's voice crackled over the airwaves. 'Where's Marshall? Is he with you now?'

'I'm here,' Richard said.

'Does it look absolutely certain that we've drawn a blank?'

' 'Fraid so.'

'Have you explored every possibility?'

'Yes.'

'Then, that's that.' The air waves crackled again until Sir James went on, 'Karen, you may as well get back here as soon as you can. There's no point in hanging around there.'

'If you don't mind, Sir,' Karen broke in, 'I'd like to take some days off if that's all right with

63

you.'

There was a brief pause as her director mulled over her request, then he said with a chuckle. 'Yes, of course it's all right. Why not? You've earned a bit of a break even if things have not turned out as we'd have hoped. Will a week be long enough?'

'A week would be fine, thanks, Sir James.'

'Well, give me a ring when you're ready to come back. Lovell's doing his best with the Wittan claim so we are managing. Enjoy yourself.' There was a click and Sir James switched off.

'He took that very well,' Richard said. 'You'd never think he'd just lost a small fortune.'

'I hope he understands my reasons for not going back to London straight away Do you think the other boat was listening in?'

'If they're who I think they are I'd bet my shirt on it. But that doesn't mean they believe us.'

'What do we do now? Stay here?'

Richard glanced through the porthole at the other boat lying so near yet so far from *Bonny Bride*. 'No, we won't be staying here.'

'Have you any plan in mind?'

'Perhaps.'

'Good. I want to finish this and get back to London as soon as I can.'

He threw her a quick glance. 'Back to civilisation? And Malcolm?'

'Of course. I have things . . .'

'Spare me the details,' Richard said curtly. They were still standing close together by the radio and as if suddenly realising this, Richard moved away briskly.

Karen moved to make some more coffee while Richard pored over the sketch of the site. 'What's your plan?'

'I don't think you're going to like it.'

'That doesn't surprise me at all.'

Despite himself, Richard smiled. But it was only for an instant. His face settled into a grave, humourless expression, and after a moment he said, quietly, 'There's only one thing we can do.' Then he went on to explain what he had in mind.

Karen's face was pale under her tan when he'd finished. She tried hard to think of an alternative to it, but couldn't.

'Do you think they'll swallow it?' she said at length.

Richard shrugged. 'I don't see why not.'

His plan had confused her more than she cared to admit, but she nodded all the same, 'If it's the only way . . .'

'It is, so there's no point in arguing about it.' After another moment or two, he added, 'How about some breakfast?'

She realised just how hungry she was after all. She set about grilling several rashers of bacon while Richard went back up on deck to furl the sails and check the engine; and to keep an eye on the other boat.

When they'd eaten, Karen stacked the dirty dishes on to the tray.

'What do you suggest we do for the rest of the day?' she asked, not looking at him.

Richard shrugged. 'Play at being tourists.'

For the next few hours they lay about the deck, sunbathing and reading. After lunch, Richard set out a couple of fishing rods, and they found themselves trying their luck. He caught a couple of mackerel and Karen promised to cook them later for supper. Then he announced he'd decided to go for a swim.

He dived from the stern and swam around, occasionally diving under the boat as though checking out the hull, but in truth, he was warming up for later that night when he would carry out his plan.

They watched the sun go down at last. The launch hadn't stirred from her anchorage all day, and all they had seen of the men on board, was an odd glimpse if one came up on deck.

'Do you really think we'll get away with it?' Karen asked as Richard prepared himself.

'Have you thought of anything better?'

She shook her head, and in a low voice she murmured, 'No.'

They waited until the dusk, not leaving it until the light had gone completely, then Richard swung himself into the wheelhouse and turned on the engine. The dull throb seemed deafening as Karen stood by the rail, staring at the launch. She could see nothing except the faint white glint of its hull as it rose and fell with the current.

The *Bonny Bride* inched slowly away into the twilight, setting a course for Gwyn Radyr Fawr. Richard maintained the pressure on the boat's throttle, guiding her through the moving patches of deeper darkness away from the launch.

They were less than a mile away from the launch when a light shone from its port bow. The light circled in the direction of where *Bonny Bride* had anchored just a few tense minutes ago, then a man appeared, a big man who ran along the launch's deck quickly, only to disappear below a few moments later.

Richard paused, watching the man's movements sharply. A look of recognition caused him to ease his grip for a moment.

She heard his gasp of surprise and she looked up in quick alarm. 'Did you know that man?' she asked in a whisper.

'Almost certain of it.'

The *Bonny Bride* lurched as though sensing the tension, and Richard gathered himself for the effort to turn the wheel quickly to starboard.

'They'd have seen us by now, wouldn't they?' she asked when they were almost clear of the other boat. 'The man must have been on watch.' Her eyes felt dry. She realised she had been staring so hard, she'd hardly blinked.

'If I'm any judge of men at sea, they're probably bored out of their minds by now, especially if they think they're on a wild goose chase,' Richard replied. 'Let's hope they've all kept off the vino and are wide awake, and let's keep our fingers crossed that they'll believe we're making for home. I don't want to blow this chance—we're running out of time.'

Karen close her eyes for an instant, then opened them again. Nothing had changed. She and Richard were still on the yacht, heading away from a launchful of bad guys. She gave a small nervous laugh. 'I feel as if I'm in a James Bond film.' She giggled softly. 'I can't believe this is really happening.'

Richard, turning his head sideways to face her, said, 'I bet you don't have as much fun as this with your bowler-hatted boyfriend!'

Karen didn't rise to his bait. Then his banter faded as he saw the hint of fear in her eyes, and how whitely her knuckles showed through the skin of her hands as they gripped hold of the rail. He switched on the automatic pilot and moved to her side.

'Karen, don't be scared,' he murmured softly, holding out his arms. 'If they're after anything at all, it's the money, not us.'

She went into his arms without hesitation, nestling up against him like a small animal seeking shelter. He drew her closer, holding her tightly. He murmured again against her hair, 'They won't hurt us.'

She nodded against his chest and said something he couldn't catch, but it sounded like his name. After a few moments he broke away and they stood apart, neither looking at the other.

'Come on,' he said quietly, 'I need some help with the navigation.'

He didn't. He knew these waters well, and Karen knew that. She also knew that he was merely trying to occupy her, take her mind off the men in the launch until they were well out of sight.

She followed Richard into the wheelhouse and they set the course for home. His right hand rested on the wheel and the other held loosely around Karen's slender shoulder. He threw a glance down in her direction. 'Feel better now?'

'I was being silly, I don't know what came over me,' she returned steadily, then she gave a small choky laugh, 'I'll be fine.'

'I know you will,' he said softly.

'Who was the man?' Karen asked after a few moments. 'You know him?'

'Yes, I think I do.'

Richard's tone wasn't exactly brusque, but he seemed to be making sure that he had his facts absolutely right.

'I'd rather not say until I can prove it.'

'Why? Don't you trust me?'

Richard turned his head to her. 'Of course I

do, it's just that there's no point in saying anything to anyone unless I'm right.' He changed the subject abruptly and stood away from the wheel. 'Here . . . want to take over for a while?'

'You're joking!' she exclaimed, looking with alarm at the complicated array of dials on the control panel.

He laughed at her wide-eyed surprise. 'It's perfectly safe, she's on automatic pilot.' He held out his hand, grasping hers in its firm grip.

'Do you trust me with her?'

He answered mildly, 'She's computerised. All you have to do is log in the course and the computer takes care of everything.'

She turned her head to look at the controls. Her green eyes scanned the instruments but when she spoke her voice was taut, 'If you have a sophisticated thing like this, why do you need sails?'

Richard smiled easily. He seemed pleased with her interest in his pride and joy. 'Because I enjoy the pleasure of taking on the wind and sea without any help from hi-tech, although it's useful in a situation like this.'

She nodded. There was still a hint of daylight in the midsummer sky. It was beautiful. Rose-red fingers streaked across the horizon and there was silence—except for the sound of the sea around them. Richard left her for a few moments and went below. When he came back he was carrying two steaming mugs of coffee and he handed her one. 'Here, drink this, it'll warm you up.'

'I'm not cold, but thanks anyway.' She clasped her hands around the mug and took a sip. It tasted good. After a few moments she asked, 'What time is it?'

Richard glanced at his watch and answered, 'A little after ten o'clock. We'll change our course in an hour. I'll take over now. You go below and have something to eat. We have a long day ahead of us tomorrow—'

Karen shook her head firmly. 'I'm not hungry.'

He shrugged nonchalantly and Karen studied his granite-hard face in the grey shadow of the wheelhouse. 'I only hope we can find the place again without too much trouble. You realise we'll have to tackle the dive from the other side of Gwyn Radyr Fach,' he muttered.

'If we estimate the bearings to be three miles off the chart's positions, we shouldn't be too far out,' she pointed out.

Richard gave a quick nod. 'Yes, but navigation can be dodgy at the best of times around these islands.'

'Why is that?'

'The currents are always uncertain—the weather, too. It can change quickly. One minute the sky can be blue and clear with perfect visibility, then suddenly a black squall can come out of nowhere.' After a few moments, Richard gave a short, mirthless laugh. 'I'd give anything to see the faces on that little lot when they turn up at Gwyn Radyr Fawr tomorrow morning and realise we've not gone back there after all.'

Karen looked up. There was no softness in his expression now, no gentleness. Only a grim determination to tack *Bonny Bride* on to a new course and finish the job they had started out to do. He looked at her briefly, then he turned away and headed the yacht swiftly through the inky black waters.

CHAPTER SIX

They sailed until the daylight had completely gone. Then Richard, giving Karen the order to douse all the lights, changed course. The darkness was total by the time they doubled back, keeping a distance of 10 miles or so from the launch. He'd hauled down the sails in order to cut down any recognition of their passing, and they both hoped fervently that the distance between them obliterated any sound.

It was a tense manoeuvre, but thankfully, without any sign of movement from the launch, they rounded the headland to reach the other side of the tiny islet of Gwyn Radyr Fawr. The rocky coastline blurred before them and the surging breakers pounded relentlessly against the jutting sides of the cliffs.

Using his sonar, Richard navigated *Bonny Bride* in through two projecting rocky outcrops of the natural harbour, guiding her expertly towards a suitable mooring.

'I think we can risk a light now. It'll be some time before it dawns on them they've been hoodwinked,' he said, cutting the motor. 'We've got at least six hours' headway, and I don't think they'll twig we've come back here until daylight.'

'Do you think they'll try to find us?'

'Probably.' He turned around and looked at

her. 'You look tired,' he said gently. 'You'd better get some rest before we do anything else.'

'I'm not tired,' she said quickly. But he was right, she suddenly felt exhausted.

'In that case, you can take this rope and find somewhere to tie us up while I finish off a few things here.'

Karen nodded. Picking up the rope and then swinging over the side of *Bonny Bride*, she waded ashore. She groped her way along the sand. There was no moon, and as she moved about the shingle of the beach, she could feel the pebbles against her bare feet, still warm from the day's hot sun. Soon her eyes grew accustomed to the darkness and it wasn't long before she found a rock to tie up *Bonny Bride*.

Back on board, she checked the bow and stern anchors while Richard ran a second line to the mooring and furled the sails more tightly to the masts. When they had finished, they went below deck and secured all the loose fittings and drawers, and when Richard was satisfied that all was well, he seated himself at the table in the galley and switched on the radio, and tuned in to the weather forecast.

'Heavy seas and gale-force winds up to fifty knots increasing,' Richard repeated after listening to the bulletin. 'The next report will be in fifteen minutes.'

Richard acknowledged the warning with a faint smile. 'Well, that's that!' he conceded.

'Looks like we won't be going anywhere for a while.'

Karen looked at him uneasily, moistening her lips with her tongue, 'Stormy weather ahead?' she asked.

'Looks like we're in for a blow,' he muttered.

'Perhaps it won't last long.' she said, her tone expressing more optimism than she felt.

After a moment's consideration Richard nodded. 'Perhaps. But then again it could be hours, or even days.'

There wasn't very much they could do about it anyway, she thought, and Karen moved across the cabin and stowed the charts into the drawer. She turned to Richard, 'How about some coffee?'

'Good idea.'

'I wonder what Malcolm would think if he could see us now,' he said as she filled the kettle. 'Marooned in a storm, miles away from anywhere.' There was a pause while he waited for her comments and when she didn't reply he went on, 'I wonder how he would handle a situation like this?'

She gave a light, choking laugh. No matter how she stretched her imagination, she couldn't see Malcolm in this situation, but loyally she responded, 'I'm sure he'd handle it very well.'

Richard gave a sort of grunt which made Karen look at him sharply, but he said no more as he sipped his coffee.

They sat in silence for a while until Karen remarked, 'Are we in for a rough night?'

'There's no need to be worried about it. We're well sheltered here, you'll hardly feel the boat move. She hasn't let me down yet.'

She looked at him with widening eyes. 'You're serious, aren't you?'

'About what?'

'*Bonny Bride* not letting you down. You really do prefer to be here on board her than on land.' It was more of a statement than a question.

'Yes. she's my life,' he admitted. 'But if it makes you nervous, we'll go back.'

Karen knew that was a challenge. He was testing her. 'I'll stay, but I think you're mad. So, what do we do? Sit and look at each other all night?'

He raised one eyebrow and grinned broadly. 'Any suggestions?'

'Yes, for a start I'll make something to eat, it's going to be a long night.'

Later, as they sat together, Richard took her hand and said softly, 'Karen, for the first time in my life I wish I was a different person. I wish I was someone else . . .'

'But you're not,' she murmured.

'I wish I was someone . . . stable, someone who . . .'

'I know . . .' Karen broke off, not looking at him. She knew exactly what he was thinking

76

and it filled her with regret.

'The thing is,' he went on, 'if we go on the way we're going, it's going to be very hard to say goodbye at the end of all this.'

She knew then he was letting her know that he didn't want to risk falling in love with her.

'I know exactly what you mean,' she murmured, staring hard into her brandy. 'You don't have to spell it out. Sometimes it's very hard to control our emotions.'

'You're getting into my system, Karen, and this isn't the best time for me to begin to care for someone.'

Looking up, she met his eyes, 'Would there ever be a best time for you?'

He shrugged, 'I doubt it. But I think you know what's happening . . .'

She knew only too well what was happening. But they were from two different worlds, and would never have met, but for a quirk of fate. Once this job was completed, they would go their own ways again. She would go back to her comfortable existence with Malcolm, and Richard would be free to follow his dreams. Her heart shied from that reality. She sensed that the pain of the parting would be too hard to bear.

Morning came at last, and with it the end of the storm. Through the porthole, Karen looked out at Gwyn Radyr Fach. It was beautiful. Birds fluttered and the flowers were a blaze of colour everywhere, and in their sheltered spot by overhanging clifftops, she could smell the sharp tang of the sea, and the delicate sweetness of the wild flowers cascading down the grey-white cliffs like brightly-coloured waterfalls.

She lay back against the pillow and closed her eyes. The insides of her lids burned. After a few moments she forced her eyes open and looked out over the bay again. How much longer would it take them to finish this job? Two more days? Three? Perhaps longer if the men in the launch were after the coins as well.

She lost track of time lying there, staring, but not seeing anything. A big white moth had blundered through the open porthole and was beating itself crazily against the wall beside her. She felt as though her heart was beating like the moth. Picking up a tissue she caught it and, reaching her arm through the opening, watched as it fluttered into the sky.

Rousing herself, she dressed quickly and went into the galley to make some sandwiches. Richard was waiting for her when she carried the tray on deck and they ate them quickly, washing them down with scalding coffee.

'We'll have to haul this stuff over the top,' Richard uttered. 'Do you think you can manage it?'

She stared at him, 'Of course I can manage it,' she said patiently, 'but, why can't we go round by the beach—it'd save the climb.'

'The beach, as you optimistically call it, runs

out around that bend. It's nothing but sheer rock until you reach the other side. We'd never make it that way without *Bonny Bride*.'

Karen absorbed this information then conceded with a small shrug.

Although the stormy rain had abated, the wind had picked up while they'd been asleep. The tops of the mountains of the mainland were wreathed in heavy mist, and the sea below was becoming choppy.

Karen shivered a little, 'The sky still looks heavy over the sea.'

He nodded. 'Yes, the weather's broken. Are you ready? We've got quite a trek in front of us to reach the other side, especially carrying the diving gear.'

'Yes, I'm ready.' she replied, following him down the stairway and picking up her equipment.

Richard led the way from *Bonny Bride* and across the pebbly sand until they reached a narrow track which led upwards to the top of the cliffs. As they reached the bottom of the cliffs, a helicopter came from the north side, not very low, and floated above them without appearing to pay them much attention.

They watched it fly south and Richard said a little sombrely, 'Whoever they are, they're out early. I'm a little curious as to who they can be.' Something in his tone caused her to glance quickly at him.

'So am I. What do you think they're looking

for?'

He spoke with a rush. 'I shouldn't think it would be us—no one knows we're here, I hope.' But he was frowning as he watched it fly off.

Karen sat down on a fallen piece of amber rock and looked around. The little island was beautiful. Sea birds circled above their heads, swooping and diving over the high, wind-hewn cliffs. Fronds of ferns and carpets of moss lent a softness to each craggy niche and crevice. She closed her eyes, listening to the screams of the gulls and enjoying the respite of the island's tranquillity.

Karen opened her eyes with a start. Richard was standing over her, frowning a little. 'What's the matter?' he said again, 'aren't you well?'

In spite of the frown, Karen heard the tone of reluctant consideration in his voice and she smiled a little. 'I'm all right,' she answered crisply. 'I was just thinking how lovely it is.'

Richard raised an eyebrow, and the corner of his mouth twitched upwards in a smile, 'I agree, it is lovely. But we're not here to enjoy the scenery. Come on, let's get going.'

They set off upwards. It was good to walk on terra firma again. The unexpected respite of a day on land buoyed Karen's spirits and the two of them made their way along the narrow tracks of the tiny islet of Gwyn Radyr Fach.

CHAPTER SEVEN

The climb up the cliff face was only a short distance and, in spite of the weight of the diving gear, they reached the top in less than half an hour. A stiff breeze was blowing in from the sea and as they paused for breath, Karen could see the bright colours of *Bonny Bride* bobbing away at anchor below them.

They set off along the wind-blown stretch of sparse grassland, their sandalled feel making a crunching sound on the path. As they walked Karen was struck again by the beauty of the island.

She stole a glance at Richard's profile, with its expression of grim determination. He managed a smile. 'If the coast's clear when we get to the other side, I'll dive straight away, conditions are just about right,' Richard commented, 'and, with a bit of luck, we'll find it.'

Although the wind was strong, the sun was blinding. Richard was already striding away and it was obvious to her that he was enjoying every minute of this. He sounded excited, amused, and not at all worried. She found herself heartened by his manner—his sense of adventure was beginning to appeal to her, too. Her nerves were already beginning to stretch expectantly and she looked at him with new eyes as she hurried alongside. There was no need to doubt him. He hadn't made any mistakes yet, had he?

They walked on for a further fifteen minutes or so towards the summit, and soon they reached the crest of the island. Through his binoculars, Richard scanned the landscape and the miles of clear, blue sea. There was no sign of anything. The men in the launch were probably far away by now. Perhaps their suspicions about them had been wrong after all.

'The coast looks clear enough,' Richard said, throwing her a quick glance.

They scrambled down the cliff face until they reached a spot where, if they had estimated the location correctly, the underwater caves lay less than half a mile away, just off the headland.

They began to strip off. Richard's fine drawn mouth lifted at the corner with a smile. 'You don't have to dive, it's quite a swim even before we find the right place. I can handle it.'

'I know you can, but I want to.'

This time they both wore wet suits, and their equipment was one oxygen bottle each, the torch, and a length of rope. Richard waded out towards the rocks with Karen following behind. Then, at his sign, they swam out towards the spur of cliff which made up the headland. Once there, they dived.

They swam deep. The water was colder than

Karen had imagined. She breathed deeply through her mouthpiece and prayed that she wouldn't get cramp. They swam deeper and deeper until they reached the caves lying below the other side of Gwyn Radyr Fach.

As they approached one particular cave, the one which the charts and photographs revealed signs of disturbance, Karen could see that the wreck of a ship—maybe even the *Tudor Warrior* herself—was lying directly across the narrow entrance. There was little left to recognise what had once been a proud ship. It had been mostly eaten away by years of immersion in the salt water of the Bristol Channel. And if it was the *Warrior* then it must have drifted the several miles from Cardigan Bay before it finally came to rest in this dark and silent place.

It was the nearest Karen had ever been to a shipwreck before, and as she swam closer, she could see the damage that had been done through long years of lying helplessly at the mercy of the sea. The yawning hole where the ship had foundered against the shelving bedrock was still clearly visible along its rotting hull.

Silvery-green forms darted about everywhere, in every nook and cranny, in and amongst the once-bright fittings of the old ship. Algae covered the rusting cannons, and every type of sea creature had adopted the wreck as their own.

Karen didn't have long to take in all this before Richard flashed the powerful beam of the torch, motioning her to follow him. He negotiated the tortuous route between the sides of the cave and the old ship's wrecked companionway. The prow of the ship was up-ended, sticking up like a macabre jagged finger, blocking the entrance to the cave. There was a tense moment when her oxygen bottle jammed against the side of the cave's jagged wall as she squeezed her way through, and it took several precious minutes before Richard was able to dislodge it. Once through, a clear passage lay ahead.

The sound of her own heartbeat was loud in her ears as she followed Richard. Everything looked ghostly. She kept directly behind him as they swam faster now inside the cave, and while they hadn't expected the chest to be standing in some easy place waiting for them, she hadn't bargained on it being so difficult to reach.

She followed Richard upwards into the gloomy darkness, the murky light giving everything around them a sensation of unreality.

Richard pointed to something above her head. She looked up but there was nothing but darkness around her. She swam upwards, following him and at last she saw it. A single casket. It was lodged on a craggy shelf, almost concealed from view at the topmost point of the cavern, heavily chained and encrusted with barnacles. A perfect hiding-place.

Richard waved her forward and, like two strange fish suspended in midstream, the two of them scraped and peeled away at the dense covering of crustation until at last, between them, they managed to clear most of the debris covering it.

It was painfully slow work, and Richard tapped the watch on his wrist, signalling for them to get a move on as the air in the cylinders was running low. They dislodged the chest. It wasn't very big; about the size of an old-fashioned briefcase, but it was heavy. Richard tied the rope as securely around it as he could and attached it to his waist, then he signalled for her to get behind him and they began the slow return to the surface.

They were both exhausted when they reached the beach. The casket was heavier than they'd imagined, and when it no longer had the buoyancy of the water to support it, it seemed to weigh a ton.

Richard hauled it ashore and Karen knelt beside him as he tried to prize open the lid with his bare hands.

'It's going to be difficult to open,' he muttered, 'I think we'll need something stronger than muscle.'

They struggled with the casket for several minutes, both of them dripping like beached dolphins and with only their swimsuits as covering. Thin rivulets of water ran from Richard's powerful body on to the sand beside her, and after a little while he flopped down and turned his head, smiling at her tangled hair.

'You did well down there. I'm impressed,' he murmured gently. 'There's more to you than meets the eye.'

'What did you expect me to do? Panic at the first sight of a fish?'

He grinned and stretched out his legs, silvery grains of sand clinging to his skin. 'Karen I've been thinking . . .'

She sat down beside him, turning her head, a smile playing around her mouth. 'Don't tell me,' she mocked. 'You've changed your mind again and you've decided to put the casket back into the sea. You said you'd been thinking.'

Richard sat up, 'Oh, that.' He inhaled deeply, as though struggling to clear his mind. He ran his hands through his hair then lay back again, propping his head upon his elbow and looking out to sea. 'It wasn't anything very much,' he murmured at last. 'Just something about . . . us.'

She glanced at him somewhat warily, asking quietly, 'What about us?'

He leaned towards her, cupping her chin with a light touch of his hand and forcing her to look at him. His face relaxed into a smile and he stroked away a strand of tawny hair that had blown across her cheek. 'We've shared a lot since we met, haven't we?'

Karen smiled back and said softly. 'Yes, I suppose we have.'

'We make a good team.'

'I suppose we do.'

The thoughts stirring in her head made her dizzy and she closed her eyes. Adventure, laughter, perhaps danger, and most of all, a kind of love—if that's what this surging of emotion really was. Yes, they'd shared a great deal and they did make a good team; they could face anything together. The thought of it was like a gnawing pain eating away at her.

'It's meant a great deal to me, Karen,' Richard murmured.

She waited, but after some moments, Richard turned away again and was looking speculatively out over the horizon. Looking for what? His freedom? His independence?

She wanted to lift her hand to his face, to trace the firm line of his jaw, darkened now by another day's growth of beard.

Richard cleared his throat, turned and smiled slightly, then said a little shakily. 'Feel rested enough? Ready to have a go at getting that thing back to the boat?' He stretched and stood up, then holding out an arm, he pulled her to her feet.

Between them they hauled the heavy casket up the cliff. Richard's rock-strong arms and hands, toughened by years of hard, physical work, seemed to make the task look so easy. And yet, as Karen helped him strain the rope for the last few yards as they reached the top, she knew those arms were also utterly gentle.

'The next bit should be easy,' he said a little out of breath. 'Karen, you carry the wet-suits and the rope—we can leave the air tanks here and pick them up later. I'll fasten the box across my back. Can you give me a hand?'

They set off again across the crest of the tiny island, stopping every now and then to shift the weight of their loads, and to regain their breath. The trek took a little over an hour and neither of them were sorry when, at last, they were safely back on board *Bonny Bride*.

They stowed away the gear then went below into the galley. Karen closed the door softly behind her and moved quietly to Richard's side. It was the moment they had both worked so hard for, the reason why they were here, and as she waited for Richard to open the casket she held her breath.

It sat darkly secretive on the table, as though reluctant to reveal its long-hidden contents. Made of lacquered teak, and in spite of its long submersion in the cold water, it was clear that it had once been quite beautiful in itself.

Using a wire cutter, Richard easily snapped off the rusted chains, and then, taking a crow bar, he started on the lid. After a few tense moments of gentle coaxing, it at last started to give.

As Richard opened the contents to the cold light of day for the first time in over five hundred years, Karen inhaled sharply. She had seen many treasures before in her line of work, but never had she been prepared for anything like this. The coins glistened dully in the soft light, thousands of them, reminding her of shards that had somehow broken away from the sun. They were perfect. These small pieces of precious circular metal were literally worth their weight in gold alone, let alone their rarity value.

Richard whistled softly. 'It's easy to see why some people go to the lengths they do to possess things like them. They're beauties.'

Karen nodded and ran her fingers through the golden hoard. 'I would estimate at least two million pounds at today's value—probably even more. It's hard to believe they've survived so long in such conditions—they're perfect.'

'Well, at least Sir James will be pleased. He'll recoup all his expenses and then some.'

'And don't forget your own expenses, they must run into a pretty penny or two by now, plus your twenty-five thousand fee.'

'Money's never meant that much to me, except for the freedom it brings. My freedom is the most precious thing in the world to me.'

She gave him a long look, trying to read his expression and finding it impossible to do. But his words were his confirmation of what she'd believed all along. This was what it had all been for. This was what he'd worked for. All the risks were to ensure his freedom. The freedom that was so precious to him. That was all that mattered.

She pushed the thought aside and concentrated on more immediate matters. 'Shall we radio Sir James straightaway and let him know of his good fortune?'

'No. we'll do that from Gwyn Radyr Fawr. Let's get out of here.'

Between them they lifted it from the table and Richard stowed the casket into the safe. It only just fitted the narrow compartment behind the bar in the main cabin, then they went on deck and prepared to set sail. Within an hour they were on their way.

Once clear from the mooring and making for the open stretch of water between themselves and Gwyn Radyr Fawr, Karen looked back at the tiny islet. The job was almost done, the Tudor treasure had been found at last and was safely stowed below. Soon it would be in the hands of her company and Sir James, and she and Richard would be saying their goodbyes. All that was left was this final mad dash back to the island.

She suddenly felt tired. The long haul over the rough ground and the deep, tense dive into the cavern were beginning to take their toll. She looked up when, she heard Richard calling her name. 'We've got company.'

Karen lifted her eyes to the sky, following his pointing thumb. A light plane had swept down from the clouds and was flying low over *Bonny Bride*, turning and spiralling in a search pattern and almost touching the topmast as it dipped down over the boat.

'Do you think they're looking for us?' she asked over the noise of the aircraft.

Richard shrugged. 'We'll have to assume so,' he replied grimly, 'don't look up—don't let them think we're concerned.'

They kept their heads down for a further five minutes, until the plane finished circling, then with a final sweep, it climbed again and headed away. Once it had disappeared from sight she said, 'What do you think that was about?'

'Who knows? But we must assume that it was our friends from the launch and that they know we have the coins.'

She paused, indecisive and exasperated. 'So, what do you suggest we do now?'

'Get on the radio to Sir James. Don't tell him we've found the coins but tell him to get someone to meet us at Gwyn Radyr. I've a feeling we'll need all the help we can use once we're back on land.'

Karen disappeared below while Richard opened up the throttle of the engine and gave *Bonny Bride* all she'd got. It was about 15 kilometres to Gwyn Radyr Fawr and Karen found herself sweating a little for fear of what might be waiting for them as they headed south-eastwards.

She made the call and went back on deck. Richard was standing by the rail scanning the sea through the binoculars. When he heard her come up beside him he lowered the glasses and said softly, 'I don't know, Karen . . . I honestly don't know.' His fingers gently read her face, not missing a detail. 'I used to have my life under control I always knew exactly what I wanted—and deep down I know I still do.' His eyes threw a dark challenge. 'Nothing and nobody is going to come between me and my life.'

Karen was intrigued. 'You're afraid I might lure you into something you'll regret?' She softly kissed the top of his finger as it rested against her lips then, a note of scepticism crept into her voice, she asked, 'Are you saying now that I'm a nothing or nobody?'

He smiled, his teeth even and white against his tanned face, 'You were a couple of weeks ago.'

A quietness came over him, settling into a long silence. It wasn't a heavy or uncomfortable silence, it was thoughtful and a little emotional. Then Richard turned his head to look out over the sea. There was no smile on his face, but Karen could sense the immense willpower that had slowly fused through his body.

She sighed. Why wouldn't he let go? Was he so afraid of admitting that he cared for her? Wait a minute . . . she was forgetting herself again. She was forgetting that she belonged to someone else . . .

Richard switched off the automatic pilot and returned the controls to manual. He looked back over his shoulder at the flapping sails.

'Karen, can you handle the wheel? I'll have to tighten that mainsail or we'll be in trouble when we turn into the wind.'

'Of course,' She moved quickly into the wheelhouse as Richard strode down the deck. Through the reflection she saw him lean forward and grab the heavy ropes, and she heard his sound of annoyance as one of them slipped wetly from his hands.

Karen kept her eyes forward, concentrating on the set course towards the island. Suddenly, she heard Richard's loud yell. The urgency of alarm in his voice made her turn quickly and, as she did, she saw the boom of the mainsail swing round completely out of control, crashing against Richard's head and throwing him heavily down on to the deck.

'Richard!' she cried.

There was no response. Fear gripped her as she saw him lying in a crumpled heap on the deck, an ugly spurt of blood springing from his forehead.

The brief spell of panic that darted through

her was quickly dispelled as she sized up the situation in a matter of seconds. She took a quick, steadying breath and switched back on to automatic, then ran down to Richard's side and, kneeling, she bent anxiously over his prone body.

He was unconscious. The boom had caught him heavily on the temple. Karen could feel her heart pounding painfully as she stroked his head, trying not to hurt him even more as she dabbed away at the rivulets of blood that were running down on to his cheek.

He stirred and opened his eyes.

'Oh, thank God, I thought . . .'

'What . . . happened . . . ?'

'Don't move. It was the boom . . . you've had a bad knock. Keep still, lie back and don't move your head.'

His eyes closed again and he groaned. She must make him comfortable and get him to hospital as quickly as possible.

She raced down to her cabin and brought up a couple of blankets and a pillow laying it gently under his head and covering him warmly.

'Karen . . .'

'Don't try to speak.'

Karen pressed her fingers gently against his lips, 'I'll get us home, Richard. Just stay quiet, please.'

His eyes closed heavily and with a soft moan he lost consciousness again. Her face was ashen as she tucked the blankets more tightly around him. She had to leave him where he lay; it was impossible to move him, and to do so would probably have caused even more harm.

It was only when she was quite sure there was nothing more she could do for him that Karen stood up. She looked around a little wildly and an ugly fear gripped her heart. There was at least another ten miles of ocean between them and safety, and with Richard lying hurt and unconscious at her feet, there was no-one else but herself to get them back.

She fought to bring her fears under some semblance of control. There was no point at all in just standing there waiting for a miracle. Slowly, commonsense took over and suddenly she was in control, and the first thing she knew she must do was to be sure that help would be at hand as soon as possible. She went back below and radioed a message to Gwyn Radyr House.

Mrs Williams took the call, and soon Karen's gasping message slowly became clear to the housekeeper. At first, the woman's agitation as she heard of the accident threatened to waste precious time and Karen broke in quickly, 'Yes, call a helicopter . . . and contact the hospital—Richard needs treatment as soon as we come in . . . tell then he's had a bad blow to his head.'

'Oh. you poor thing, you can't sail *Bonny*

Bride all by yourself—I'll get the launch out to you right away . . .'

'If you like, but please telephone the hospital first. I'll talk to you later . . .'

She replaced the mouthpiece and ran back on deck. She gave another glance towards Richard, her heart aching to see him lying there so helpless, and then she drew a long breath and prayed, 'Don't let me down, *Bonny Bride*, please don't let me down.'

Karen secured the still-flapping boom as tightly as she could. What strength she had was no match for the heavy boom and before long she was panting heavily as she pulled on the wet ropes. The effort took some time but in the end she managed it. Once she was satisfied that it would hold, at least until they reached land again, she ran back to the wheelhouse, and with shaking hands she switched back to manual.

Karen gritted her teeth. Her jaw was already aching with the tension and she turned her concentration on the electronic panel by the wheel. She set the course, sending up a fervent prayer as she did so. Then, taking a long breath, she tapped the walnut casing of the panel and uttered, 'It's up to us now *Bonny Bride*. Don't let me down. If you love him as much as I do, then help me get him home. . .'

It took all of Karen's strength to keep her on course and heading for home, but soon the yacht settled down, and Karen was able to hold her steady. The smooth hull cut swiftly through the water and ploughed a white trough between the waves.

They headed east and, after a while Karen began to breathe more evenly; in spite of everything, she found herself savouring the feeling of being part of something much more powerful than herself.

Soon the grey-green smudge that was Gwyn Radyr Fawr was clearly in sight. All that she could do now was to keep her cool for the remaining few miles.

The headland lay before her and the wind cut across *Bonny Bride* like a living thing. It cracked against the furled sails as if challenging both Karen and the boat to defy it, lifting and lowering the bow as if it was a toy puppet that had lost its strings. Heavy spray lashed the wheelhouse, throwing a spume of inpenetrable drizzle against the shielding glass in front of her, but Karen knew once she'd turned the headland, they would be home and dry.

CHAPTER EIGHT

Karen stared grimly out at the heaving waves, thankful for the computer keeping her on course. She'd covered about half the distance, but suddenly her heart leapt with relief as she saw the launch.

She grabbed the binoculars and focused them on the grey ocean. It looked just a little like a bobbing orange on the crest of the waves at first, and seemed so tiny and vulnerable against the heavy swell of the sea, that she was afraid it would swallow it up. But it was getting closer every second and on its way to help them.

Karen slowed *Bonny Bride* down and let down the stern anchor as she waited. In less than 10 minutes it had come alongside, and Karen went quickly to the side-rail to catch the rope as one of the launch's crew threw it on to *Bonny Bride*'s slippery deck.

She leaned over the rail. 'Am I glad to see you!' she called through the short distance that separated them. 'I didn't expect anyone to get out here so quickly.'

Soon three men were clambering aboard and she gave a surprised laugh of relief when she recognised Mike Johnson.

Mike hauled himself up over the rail of the boat and grinned. 'I didn't expect such a welcome. What's the matter? Having a spot of trouble?'

'Yes. Do you know if the hospital's been told about us? Is the helicopter on its way?'

Two other men were now aboard and standing behind Mike. One of them, a fat man in khaki shorts, Karen remembered as one of the men she'd seen around Gwyn Radyr Fawr.

'Helicopter?' Mike's pale eyes searched her face sharply, 'I don't know anything about a helicopter. Where's Richard?'

She suddenly knew something was wrong. Her eyes widened in dismay, 'He's there . . . he's been hurt.' She pointed her hand towards Richard. Something was triggering off a warning bell somewhere inside her head. Looking at Mike Johnson, and at the two men with him, caused a terrible uncertainty to stir inside her.

She tried to throw the feeling off, She'd known Mike for years, surely he would help her?

The larger of the two men behind Mike shuffled his feet impatiently, 'Get on with it, Mike, we'd better get out of here if there's a chopper on its way.'

'Be quiet!' Mike hissed at the man, then turning back to Karen he asked, 'What's happened to him?'

'Come on,' said the smaller man. 'Let's leave it. We could be in trouble . . .'

So these people weren't here to help her

after all. They were the men from the launch, and they were here for one purpose only. They were here to steal the Tudor coins. She had to think quickly. She had to get Richard to hospital, but she also had to protect their hard-won prize.

'What are you doing here, Mike?' she asked, desperately trying to hide any sign of nervousness, 'Why have you come if not to help Richard?'

Mike Johnson looked at her narrowly, 'I think you know what we're after, Karen.'

'No, I don't.'

He shrugged, his eyes moving along the deck to where Richard lay, 'We want the Tudor gold and then we'll be on our way.'

'I don't know what you're talking about,' Karen bluffed, 'We're wasting time, Mike. I need to get Richard ashore—and quickly, as you can see.'

The big man in the khaki shorts moved menacingly closer, 'Come on, let's have a look round—we're wasting time.'

Karen stood her ground, 'You're not looking around anywhere.'

'Don't make me do something I'll regret . . .' he growled, but Mike raised his arm and prevented him getting any closer to her.

'Stop that, Frankie, there's no need to get rough,' he said sharply, then he added, 'no harm in looking around though.' The other, smaller man looked at Mike expectantly,

'Bernie, you take the stern and you, Frankie, can take the bow. I'll stay here to see that nobody interferes.'

The two men moved off and Mike braced himself against the handrail, groping into the pocket of his jacket and pulling out a cigarette. He lit it, shielding the flame against the wind with his hands and all the while keeping a close eye on Karen.

A slight frown marred Mike's narrow forehead. 'We're only after the money.' He inhaled deeply and blew out a thin column of smoke, then he said, 'We're not here to hurt either of you. Too bad about Richard. I'm sorry he's hurt. If you'll tell us where the gold is, it would save time.'

'I don't know what you're talking about . . .' She broke off, her face contorting with worry, 'How could you do this? How can you allow those men to ransack Richard's boat like this? How can you . . .'

'I've as much right to look for that treasure as you have,' he snapped. 'We know you've got it, we followed you out to Gwyn Radyr Fach. Oh, yes, you fooled us for a while with that clever little trick of doubling back, but we soon twigged when you weren't at Gwyn Radyr Fawr.'

'This is nonsense . . .'

'No it isn't. I've known about Sir James's plans for some time now and I thought I'd make a bit of money for myself—the easy way.'

101

'You're crazy . . .'

'Perhaps,' he laughed softly, 'but not so crazy as to risk my neck diving in these waters. But then, why should we when you two so kindly did all the hard work for us.'

Karen's heart pounded painfully but she managed to say calmly, 'There is no treasure—and this time you're wasting is only making it more serious for Richard. He needs a doctor . . .'

Mike turned on her harshly, 'I don't wish him any harm, Karen. Honestly.'

'Then go! Take your men and leave me alone to take him back.'

But as she spoke, the distinct sound of helicopter rotors sounded in the sky above them and, within seconds, the two men came running back on deck empty-handed. Bernie was already heading over the side and into the launch, but the bigger one in the faded khaki shorts and frayed brown shirt stood by the wheelhouse and panted. 'Come on, we'd better forget it. We can have another try later.'

Mike threw Karen a sharp glance and then looked upwards to the helicopter. He stood undecided for a moment or two then he threw away his half-smoked cigarette and moved quickly across to the side, 'Richard Marshall always did get all the luck!' he called. Then with a last look up into the sky he disappeared over the side and was gone.

The helicopter hovered above her head and

Karen watched as the two air-sea rescue men harnessed Richard on to a stretcher.

'Be careful!' Karen called out in alarm. 'He's taken quite a knock.'

'I'm a doctor,' one of the men called back. 'We'll have him in St David's within half-an-hour.'

She breathed her relief, 'Thank goodness ...' then quickly looking up into the man's face she asked anxiously, 'Will he be all right?'

He nodded, 'I should think so. I've known him since the day he was born. It'll take more than a blow on the head to finish Richard Marshall off.' Then beckoning to the two men with the stretcher he instructed, 'Right, winch him up carefully ...'

'It's OK, miss,' said the young seaman by her side, 'we'll take the *Bonny Bride* back to Gwyn Radyr.'

As the helicopter bore Richard away to hospital, Karen gladly handed over his pride and joy, slumping down in relief on a sheet of tarpaulin. Gwyn Radyr was getting closer by the minute and she couldn't remember when she had been so thankful to arrive anywhere in her life before.

Before the rescuing helicopter had arrived she'd been at the wheel for over an hour, keeping her eyes riveted on the course Richard had set, but her heart constantly with him as he lay so quietly at the other end of the deck.

The gentle bump of the hull as she edged into the tiny harbour gave her such a feeling of relief that, on impulse, she bent her head and kissed the wheel. 'Thank you, *Bonny Bride*,' she breathed. 'I knew you'd help me, I knew we'd make it.' She leaned back in the seat and rested her head in her hands out of sheer exhaustion.

Suddenly, the sudden babble of sound from the jetty caused her to jerk up her head. There were swarms of people buzzing about and she remembered Richard's warning again that there may be trouble when they arrived home. He'd been right about that, just as he'd been right about everything else.

Her eyes scanned the tiny harbour for any sign of the launch. It was there, but its deck was crowded with people looking remarkably like policemen. Of Mike and his pals there was no sign. Her throat felt dry and she had trouble swallowing as she gazed confusedly about her.

At first the only familiar face she could see belonged to Richard's housekeeper, Mrs Williams. Then, as her eyes became familiar with the scene, she recognised the bulky figure of Sir James, purple-faced, and yelling instructions to half-a-dozen men carrying ropes and other equipment, and already taking charge of *Bonny Bride*.

'Miss Muir!'

Sir James's voice was calling her, breaking

through her thoughts.

'Karen! For Heaven's sake, what's been happening here? Are you all right?'

The familiar distinguished figure of Sir James strode down the deck towards her. She turned sharply, blinking through the confusion.

'I thought you were supposed to be taking a few days' holiday.' Sir James's keen blue eyes held a look of worry as they scanned her pale face.

'What's happened to Marshall?' Sir James was abrupt, business-like, but not without concern. 'How did he hurt himself? Will somebody please tell me what's been going on?'

Karen made her decision. 'Sir James, I'm sorry but I must go . . . I've got to see Richard.' She turned quickly towards the gangway, then paused and turned back, dashing back into the wheelhouse to grab the bunch of keys in the ignition. She snatched them out, selecting one and pressing it into his hand, 'May I borrow your car?'

'My car? But of course, but why?'

She didn't let him finish as he handed her the key, 'By the way, here's the key you need, I believe you'll find what you want in the safe behind the bar.'

'The safe? But, what . . .? Where are you going now . . .?'

'To the hospital.' She was already halfway

down the steps.

'Wait a moment, won't you . . . Malcolm's here.'

She paused for a fraction of a second. 'Malcolm? Malcolm's here?'

'Yes! He's waiting for you at . . .'

Karen was no longer listening to her boss. She leapt down the last two steps of the gangplank and started to run along the jetty towards Sir James' Rolls-Royce, pushing her way through the crowd.

Sir James was still calling her, 'We're staying at the White Hart, that little place on the mainland across from the harbour . . .'

She looked back briefly and waved as he leaned over the side of the rail. 'I know it.' She gave him a final wave. 'I'll find you.' Then she sped across the grass without looking back again.

The time passed slowly in the waiting room Richard had been taken away for an X-ray and now, as the white-coated young man opened the door, she leaped to her feet to ask anxiously, 'How is he, doctor?'

The doctor's eyes were fixed on a clipboard of notes. 'There are no open wounds, no lesions, no infection as far as we can tell at this stage.' His manner was curt, professional, and polite.

She exhaled slowly. 'Thank goodness.'

The young man nodded. 'But we'd like to keep him here for a few days. He was badly concussed, you know. You can see him for a few minutes, but make sure you don't tire him.'

'I understand.'

Karen walked a little behind the doctor through a labyrinth of clinically-clean corridors until they reached a door. 'He's in here.' He opened the door letting Karen through, pausing to remind her, 'Only a few minutes I'm afraid, and not too much talking if you don't mind. No excitement of any kind.'

Karen nodded, her eyes wide as she looked across the room to where Richard lay sleeping soundly.

She moved quietly across to his bed, lifted up a chair, and set it down quietly by his side. She looked at Richard's sleeping face. His breathing was even and regular and a wide plaster covered the side of his temple where the boom had hit him. Underneath, and around the edges Karen could see the deep bluish marks that gave away the unmistakeable signs of bruising. His hair looked darker than ever against the white of the pillow, and her hands reached out, seemingly of their own accord, and rested gently on his.

At her touch he gave a small moan.

'Richard . . .' she whispered, 'Richard, can you hear me?'

He stirred and turned his head to one side. His dark eyelashes flickered momentarily and then he opened his eyes. For a brief moment he looked surprised to see her smiling down at him, but then his mouth broke into a grin as he recognised his visitor.

'Karen, you're a sight for sore eyes,' he said slowly.

'How are you feeling?'

'A bit groggy, but they assure me I'll live. What happened back there?'

'The boom . . . it swung round and caught you on the head.'

He rubbed his hand gingerly along the plaster, 'So it did. That was pretty stupid of me—never happened before.' His dark eyes looked thoughtful for a moment then he looked at Karen narrowly. 'And you brought *Bonny Bride* in single-handed?'

She looked away, suddenly self-conscious.

'Not all the way, the air sea-rescue people came out to us.'

'And the casket? Was there any trouble when you brought her in?'

'No, no trouble at all, it's quite safe. There's no need for you to worry. Sir James is here—I radioed for help remember? And when I reached the jetty half the population of Wales was waiting for us.'

He lay his head back on the pillow and looked up at the ceiling and neither spoke for several moments Then she raised her eyes to Richard to find he was looking at her with such intensity that she felt her heart miss a beat. Then he went on quietly, so quietly that she scarcely heard him. 'And you saved my life.'

She smiled softly. 'I only did what anyone would do in the same situation.'

'There's no need to feel embarrassed about it. I could have been killed,' he reminded her. 'I mean it, Karen, I'm full of admiration for the way you handled everything.'

She took a deep breath and nodded, 'There's no need for you to be. I'm used to looking after myself . . .' She broke off letting the sentence hang.

'I know you are.'

Their eyes met and they smiled at each other. It was amazing how comfortable she felt just sitting there with Richard and she let her gaze flicker over his face wondering if he felt the same. The silence was finally broken as she said a little shakily, 'Well, we did it, didn't we?'

His dark eyes held hers with a look of great gentleness. 'I told you. We're a good team.'

Karen gave him a small smile and they lapsed into silence again. She had never imagined she would ever feel such emotion.

The job was finished now. There was no reason for her to stay and the thought of it was like a knife cutting through her heart.

He stirred. 'How's *Bonny Bride*? Is she damaged?'

She looked up and studied his darkly handsome face, then abruptly turned away. 'No,' she answered softly. 'She's fine.'

'I told you she wouldn't let us down.'

She could tell by the look in his eyes that he was already back on his beloved yacht; back in his world of adventure and excitement, a world that she had been able to share for a brief time, and if he hadn't had the accident he would probably already be starting on his next speculative enterprise.

She must never let him know her feelings for him. She must make no claims on his love. It was time for her to leave.

'I'll have to go now, Richard,' she said, a note of sadness in her voice.

Richard's eyes followed her movements as she stood up. 'Will you come and see me again tomorrow?' he asked mildly.

She smiled and shook her head, her long tawny hair swinging about her shoulders. There was no point in giving away her feelings now. 'I'm going back to London tomorrow,' she told him as casually as she could. 'Sir James is here and I'm seeing him tonight. He'll probably be in to see you tomorrow.'

'Do you have to go back to London tomorrow?' A frown was darkening across his brow.

'Yes.' Her reply was little more than a whisper.

'Back to Malcolm?'

'And to my job.' She was trying her best to look nonchalant. She'd already decided she would have to break her engagement. It wouldn't be fair to marry a man she did not love.

She moved away, but as she turned he caught hold of her hand. 'Karen—'

'Yes?' she answered softly.

'Why don't you stay here.'

Her eyes widened as she heard his words. 'But—but I have to go back.'

'No, you don't. We make a good team, don't we? We could be business partners. We could build up a life together.' He seemed to be testing her, his eyes intent and questioning.

Her eyes widened incredulously. 'You're serious, aren't you?'

'Very.'

Karen looked at him for a long time, trying to see something in his eyes, his manner, other than the fact that they would make a good business partnership, but she could see nothing. She wasn't going to give herself to anyone simply by the fact that they made a 'good team'. There had to be love, too.

She withdrew her hand and took a few steps towards the door, 'I think you know my answer to that, don't you?' she asked sadly. 'Take care of yourself, Richard, and good luck.'

This time Richard didn't try to stop her. When she reached the door she turned to look at him. 'Goodbye, Richard.'

Those two words sounded so final, so hollow, that Karen felt as though her heart would burst.

He lay with his head on the pillow just watching quietly, letting her go. She gave him one last smile as she opened the door, then she went through and closed it softly behind her.

CHAPTER NINE

The church clock was striking four o'clock by the time the car pulled up outside the White Hart.

'There you are, my dear.' Sir James's well-preserved features beamed across the hotel foyer as Karen stepped inside. 'I telephoned the hospital and they tell me that Marshall is quite comfortable.'

A terrible feeling of sadness had grown inside Karen since she left the hospital. Seeing her employer stride across the floor to meet her only compounded the knowledge that she was soon to step forever out of this scene and back into her old one. Huskily, she said, 'Yes, Sir James, he's quite comfortable, I shouldn't be surprised if he wasn't sent home soon.'

'Splendid! I must pay him a visit tomorrow to thank him personally for his achievement—yours too, of course Miss Muir.'

He took her by the arm and led her into the unoccupied coffee-lounge, inviting her to sit at one of the tables and seating himself opposite.

When she was settled, Karen began to talk. In her clear voice she told him the whole story from beginning to end, keeping back nothing except her personal feelings towards Richard. It felt strange relating their fears and suspicions about the launch, and the way they'd dived into the dark, deep cave for Henry Tudor's treasure. It felt even more strange to find that she was able to tell him everything in a voice that was so completely empty of emotion.

Sir James listened to her without interruption, nodding his head now and then.

At last, Karen came to the end of her report by asking the final question. 'Did you open the safe? Did you find the casket?'

Sir James beamed. 'I certainly did. What a find! I knew my instincts were right in getting young Marshall to do the job.'

A brief surge of pride and gladness darted through her at Sir James's words, but they were quickly dispelled as he went on, 'He was right about the launch, you know.'

Karen took a quick breath. 'Yes, I know he was.' She smiled grimly, remembering Mike Johnson and the two men aboard *Bonny Bride*. 'Richard must have had an idea they were on our tail from the beginning.'

'Indeed they were. But we had an idea they might be and made sure we had all contingencies covered.'

'What . . . ?'

Sir James smiled at Karen's incredulous, wide-eyed expression and shook his silver head knowingly. 'We've had an idea about them since the operation began.'

'Then why didn't you say anything about it? Surely I—we had a right to know . . .' She broke off, her face becoming flushed as anger now took the place of incredulity.

'My motives were for the best. Let me explain.'

Sir James unfolded his story. He'd known about Mike Johnson and his plans for months, since the day he'd found him photographing the charts in the office. He'd let him go deliberately, hoping that eventually Mike would lead them to the people who were paying him.

Sir James sat back with a sigh. 'I knew you two could do it if anyone could. I've recognised your courage before, Karen, and as for Richard Marshall . . . it's a great pity there aren't more men of his capabilities around these days.'

She listened to Sir James's praises of Richard quietly. A lump was beginning to form in her throat and her heart was heavy with sadness. She could hear the clock ticking away on the old fashioned mantelshelf and her thoughts went again to Richard and what they'd been through. She was feeling exhausted with the excitement and confusion of the last few hours. He watched her from across the table.

For 65, Sir James was a handsome man. Every silver hair was in place, and his expensive suit fitted his broad frame perfectly, giving him the look of a diplomat.

He sat erect with one arm resting on the arm

of the chair, his sharp blue eyes scrutinizing her closely, then he said very quietly, 'You two seem to have got on very well . . .'

She held his gaze. Then gave a small sigh and shrugged, 'We got on well enough, I suppose.'

Suddenly she sensed rather than heard a movement behind him. Her suspicions were confirmed when she heard a slight creak on the carpeted floor. At first Sir James's heavy bulk hid the newcomer from her view, and it wasn't until the man appeared from behind a screen that Karen recognised the neat, familiar shape of her Malcolm.

Looking round, Sir James heaved himself out of the chair. 'Look who's here.' His words held a hint of wry amusement at Karen's evasive discomfort. 'I'll leave you two together. I'm sure you have a lot to talk about.'

He left the room, leaving Karen to brace herself for the painful duty which lay before her.

CHAPTER TEN

Karen stood by the window in her air-conditioned office looking down on to the hurly-burly of the traffic below. She pulled up the slatted blind to let in the afternoon sun, and looked across the park. The sun was a golden ball in the September sky, and the bright summer days she'd spent on *Bonny Bride* had given way to the softer hues of autumn.

The announcement in this morning's paper had confirmed her suspicions that Malcolm hadn't taken long to get over their broken engagement.

It was hard to believe that three months had flown by since that evening in the little hotel in Wales. Three months since she and Malcolm had split up—since they'd both gathered the courage to admit their engagement was a sham.

The announcement shouldn't have surprised her, but it did. Malcolm had finally done it. He'd married someone else. And she thought wryly, by the look of it, the marriage wouldn't harm his career either. His new wife's father just happened to be looking for a man with Malcolm s ability to run the family firm.

A small smile lifted the corners of her mouth. It had also been the same three months since she'd seen Richard. It was a little ironic that she was alone now. Alone to live her life as she wished without having to be suffocated by Malcolm or live on a knife's edge with Richard.

A small frown marred her brow as Richard's face swam into her thoughts. Apart from a bouquet of red and white roses and a single-page letter thanking her for everything, she'd heard nothing more from him. Nothing at all to let her know that he was missing her as much as she missed him. Since she'd been back she'd telephoned the hospital twice and they had told her he was well on the road to recovery; the last time she called they told her he'd already been discharged and gone home.

She'd telephoned Gwyn Radyr house once on the excuse of asking how he was, but he hadn't been there either. Mrs Williams didn't know where he'd gone—he'd mentioned something about the South of France. The only thing she'd been able to learn for sure was that he'd gone off somewhere on *Bonny Bride*, and the housekeeper didn't know when he'd be back.

She turned away from the window and sat at her desk, folding the newpaper and placing it into the wastepaper basket.

She picked up a report, letting her eyes scan the neatly-typed sheet when the voice of her secretary drifted through the open door, breaking into her thoughts. 'Someone here to see you, Karen.'

The door opened a moment later 'Hello, Karen.'

Karen's head jerked up at the sound of his voice.

He stepped forward from the shadow of the doorway. Karen's heart almost choked her with its beating as she stared unbelievingly at his familiar frame moving towards her, his lean, muscular body more attractive than ever, and those devastating night-dark eyes looking down into hers.

They were studying her reaction with such intensity that Karen found it impossible to drop her gaze.

'Richard . . .' She stared at him disbelievingly.

'What are you doing here . . . They told me you were in the South of France . . . somewhere.' She paused trying to find enough breath to continue.

'I've been waiting for something that belongs to me,' he said coldly

She took a deep breath. She could hardly believe what was happening; that he was beside her again and that it felt so good to feel him standing close to her again.

'You didn't think you were going to get away from me that easily, did you?'

Karen looked up into his face for a sign of teasing, but there was none. Her smile was a little flustered. 'I don't like surprises . . . especially with you.' She hadn't intended to be

119

so honest, but she could no longer hide the joy that his nearness brought.

She laughed softly. 'You still haven't told me what you're doing here.'

'I must give Sir James credit for that,' he said. 'He rang me last night to tell me Malcolm had married someone else.' He leaned over the desk, taking hold of her hand and kissing the tips of her fingers, then he added quietly, 'It's time we talked.'

His expression took on a more serious look and he ran his finger lightly along her cheekbone. His voice was very low as he asked, 'Is there anything important for you still in London?'

She glanced away, turning her head from his compelling and hypnotic eyes. 'Yes, Richard. I have my job . . . and my flat and friends . . .'

'I meant . . . is there *anyone* important here for you?'

She shook her head slowly and gave a small shrug of her shoulders, desperately at a loss for words. 'That would depend . . .'

'Depend on what?'

She balked the question, asking instead, 'Why didn't you answer my calls?'

'I've been away. I thought when you left me in the hospital that day that Malcolm was the one you wanted. I didn't know you'd broken with him until last night.' His eyes met hers and she could see the anguished need shining from them. 'I could make up lots of fancy words but it would all come down to the same thing. I had to make sure you want the same thing just as badly as I do,' he murmured softly.

Richard looked at her closely and Karen knew he was giving her the chance to say no. The look in his eyes told her he wanted her so much but that he would be prepared to wait a little longer if that's what she wanted.

She looked up into his eyes and what she saw there made her breath catch in her throat: passion, urgency, but something else, something much more. She saw a tenderness so great that it made her realise that she hadn't yet begun to know the depths of this man.

'How long does it take two people to realise that they love each other?' He pulled her up gently from her chair, holding her and burying his face in her long tawny hair. 'And you love me, Karen, I know you do . . .'

Karen could only stare at him, still not sure whether she was dreaming it all, 'And . . . you love me?'

Richard laughed softly. 'I've never loved anyone or anything more in my life.' Then he gave a low chuckle, a sound that was warm and husky with emotion. 'I'll have to admit though—I've fought against it.'

'Yes . . . and I've fought with my own feelings, too.'

He bent forward, smiling with infinite

tenderness and kissing her softly against her hair. 'You got under my skin and I knew I was lost . . . Then I knew that if I didn't do something soon, someone else would snap you up and I'd have lost you forever.'

He drove his hands into the soft silk of her hair, burying his face against the satiny flesh of her neck and she turned, making it easier for him to hold her against him. 'Tell me you love me,' he whispered.

Karen lifted her hand to his face. 'I love you, Richard Marshall.' She smiled, touching his lips with hers.

Richard cupped her face between his hands, his eyes smiling.

'If Malcolm hadn't met his new lady, would you have married him? Even though you knew how we felt about each other?'

'After meeting you how could I? I couldn't live a lie.'

He placed his hand over hers as she ran it along the scar on his temple. 'By the way, I didn't tell you, did I . . . ?

'Tell me what?'

'There's an old Welsh proverb that says when you've saved someone's life, you belong to them for ever.'

Karen chuckled softly. 'I've never heard of that one.'

He grinned. 'Well, I've just made it up.'

'So,' she whispered, 'you're my responsibility from now on.'

'And you're mine,' he murmured gravely, pulling her closer to him. 'The three of us—you, me and *Bride*—we'll sail the world together.'

'Sounds wonderful,' she murmured.

Richard kissed her softly on the tip of her nose. 'We'll finish off the marina and then take the trip as our honeymoon.'

Karen laughed softly, kissing him back. 'Our honeymoon?'

'I suppose we might as well get married. What do you think?'

Karen's face shone with happiness. 'I suppose we might as well . . .'

We hope you have enjoyed this Large Print book. Other Chivers Press or G.K. Hall & Co. Large Print books are available at your library or directly from the publishers.

For more information about current and forthcoming titles, please call or write, without obligation, to:

Chivers Press Limited
Windsor Bridge Road
Bath BA2 3AX
England
Tel. (01225) 335336

OR

G.K. Hall & Co.
P.O. Box 159
Thorndike, Maine 04986
USA
Tel. (800) 223-2336

All our Large Print titles are designed for easy reading, and all our books are made to last.